J BLY
Bly, Stephen A., 1944-
Hazards of the half-court
press /
32050003542286

WITHDRAWN

Haza

CROSSWAY BOOKS BY STEPHEN BLY

THE STUART BRANNON WESTERN SERIES

Hard Winter at Broken Arrow Crossing
False Claims at the Little Stephen Mine
Last Hanging at Paradise Meadow
Standoff at Sunrise Creek
Final Justice at Adobe Wells
Son of an Arizona Legend

THE NATHAN T. RIGGINS WESTERN
ADVENTURE SERIES
(Ages 9–14)

The Dog Who Would Not Smile
Coyote True
You Can Always Trust a Spotted Horse
The Last Stubborn Buffalo in Nevada
Never Dance with a Bobcat
Hawks Don't Say Goodbye

THE CODE OF THE WEST SERIES

It's Your Misfortune & None of My Own
One Went to Denver & the Other Went Wrong
Where the Deer & the Antelope Play
Stay Away From That City . . . They Call It Cheyenne
My Foot's in the Stirrup . . . My Pony Won't Stand

THE AUSTIN-STONER FILES

The Lost Manuscript of Martin Taylor Harrison
The Final Chapter of Chance McCall
The Kill Fee of Cindy LaCoste

THE LEWIS AND CLARK SQUAD ADVENTURE SERIES
(Ages 9–14)

Intrigue at the Rafter B Ranch
The Secret of the Old Rifle
Treachery at the River Canyon
Revenge on Eagle Island
Danger at Deception Pass
Hazards of the Half-Court Press

Hazards of the
Half-Court Press

STEPHEN BLY

EAST CENTRAL REGIONAL LIBRARY
244 SOUTH BIRCH STREET
CAMBRIDGE, MN 55008

CROSSWAY BOOKS • WHEATON, ILLINOIS
A DIVISION OF GOOD NEWS PUBLISHERS

Hazards of the Half-Court Press

Copyright © 1998 by Stephen Bly

Published by Crossway Books
 a division of Good News Publishers
 1300 Crescent Street
 Wheaton, Illinois 60187

All rights reserved. No part of this publication may be reproduced, stored in a retrieval system or transmitted in any form by any means, electronic, mechanical, photocopy, recording or otherwise, without the prior permission of the publisher, except as provided by USA copyright law.

Cover illustration: Sergio Giovine

Cover design: Cindy Kiple

First printing, 1998

Printed in the United States of America

Library of Congress Cataloging-in-Publication Data
Bly, Stephen, 1944-
    Hazards of the Half-Court Press / Stephen Bly.
        p.   cm.—(The Lewis and Clark Squad adventure series ; bk. 6)
    Summary: Thirteen-year-old Cody and his friends look for divine help when they face problems which divert their attention from the end-of-the-summer basketball tournament.
    ISBN 0-89107-986-6
    [1. Basketball—Fiction.   2. Christian life—Fiction.]   I. Title.
II. Series: Bly, Stephen A., 1944-   Lewis & Clark Squad adventure series ; bk. 6.
PZ7.B6275Hax 1998
[Fic]—dc21   97-32230

06		05		04		03		02		01		00		99		98
15	14	13	12	11	10	9	8	7	6	5	4	3	2	1

For my good pals
Zachary & Miranda

One

Cody Clark took the pass from Larry Lewis and tossed the basketball back out to Jeremiah Yellowboy.

"Keep the ball moving!" Feather hollered from the sideline. Her words bounced in rhythm with her black canvas high-tops and her long, wispy brown ponytail.

Over to Larry.

In to Cody.

Out to Jeremiah.

Over to Larry.

Back to Jeremiah.

Behind the three-point line.

A quick shot.

A quick three.

"All right!" Larry howled. He huddled his team quickly while the Little Creek Lions retrieved the ball that rolled toward the stage in the Halt High School gym. The Lewis and Clark Squad's bright orange, yellow, and chartreuse tie-dyed T-shirts hung like a canvas of modern art.

"Cody, you've got to take a shot inside. It's getting

harder and harder for me and Townie to see the basket on the outside. If you get clear, toss it up."

Cody glanced over his shoulder at the largest member of the Lions. "Freight Train is shoving me pretty good underneath. He won't give me much."

"With your back to the basket, fake right, go left, and bank one in. I'll follow on the left for a rebound," Larry instructed. "You always make that shot when we're playing one-on-one."

"I'll try," Cody offered. "But *you* don't weigh 200 pounds and fill the entire key."

Jeremiah pulled up his T-shirt and wiped the sweat off his forehead. "I can't believe the Lions have improved so much since we played them last."

"There are no easy games from now on. We win this, and we're in the semifinals. And if we lose . . . well, I can't even imagine that." Larry clapped his hands together several times. "Come on, guys, let's go!"

Kenny McClain drove the ball straight at Cody. When he pulled up for a jump shot, Cody leaped to block the ball. There wasn't a shot—only a fake and a bounce-pass to a back-cutting Dink Wilkins.

It was an easy lay-in.

"Feather, come in for me," Jeremiah called. "I'm not keeping up with Dink."

Dressed in jeans shorts and her tie-dyed T-shirt, Feather trotted onto the court. Her ponytail hung down her back almost to her waist.

Dink scooted over to guard her. He was a couple of inches shorter than she was, and his black hair, parted in the middle, hung almost to his eyes. "Hey, is Feather your real name or just a weird nickname?"

She took a pass from Larry, looked left, and tossed it right. "Is Dink your real name or only a statement about the size of your brain?"

Dink slammed his hands on his hips.

Larry's pass came right back to Feather, who broke around Dink and drove to the basket. Mully "Freight Train" Banks, guarding Cody, stepped out to cut her off. But instead of shooting, she bounced it in to Cody, who faked right and turned left for a hook shot.

The synthetic leather Spalding sphere crashed off the glass of the west backboard, slammed into the orange iron rim, and then bounced high into the air. The ball came down to the left of the basket. There was no way for Cody to get around Freight Train. Suddenly Larry came flying in from the three-point line, grabbed the rebound, and flipped the ball back up toward the basket.

It bounced high on the glass but dropped straight into the net. "Yes!" Larry pumped his right arm back and forth as he trotted out into position for playing defense. Cody heard most of the 200 or so people in the bleachers clap and cheer.

This time Dink dribbled back and forth above the three-point line with Feather in pursuit. "When are you and Clark getting married?" He flipped his hair out of his eyes with his left hand and dribbled with his right.

Feather kept her long, thin arms straight out to her sides as she kept between Dink and the basket. "What are you talking about?"

"Everyone in Halt knows you two are a number."

She reached in to slap the ball away. She missed. "We're only thirteen."

"Yeah, but you're, you know . . . you two have obviously been . . ."

Feather stopped her pursuit and dropped her hands to her hips. "We've obviously been what?" she demanded.

The split second of fury in her green eyes was exactly what Dink was looking for. The second she hesitated, he broke around her and drove to the basket. Cody sprinted up to block him, but Dink glanced at Freight Train, and Cody dropped back to intercept a pass that never came.

It was an easy lay-in for Dink.

"Time-out!" Larry hollered. "We want our last time-out!"

The Lewis and Clark Squad huddled around Jeremiah at the sideline. The audience shouted and clapped for the two teams. Cody glanced up to see J. J. slap a high five to Devin.

"My fault, Cody," Feather confessed. "He baited me. I don't know why I even listened to him. You three guys are the only boys in town that aren't jerks."

"We can't give them another bucket," Larry maintained. "We've got to sink one, but the big thing is to keep them from answering right back with another basket."

"Let's double-team Dink," Feather suggested.

"But that leaves someone open."

Feather bit her lip and then waved her hands in the air as she spoke. "When Dink tosses it over to Kenny, Cody will sprint out to guard him. I'll break to Freight Train and intercept the pass. I'll toss it out to Larry, while Cody breaks to the hoop."

Larry's mouth dropped open.

"What's the matter, L. B.? Didn't you think we were learning anything from you? I think Feather has a workable plan."

Larry shook his head. "If she misses the pass, they get an easy lay-in, and our season is over."

"I can do it," Feather insisted.

"Freight Train has missed lay-ins before," Jeremiah reminded them.

"But we can't count on that. Maybe I'd better go for the steal," Larry conceded.

"I said I can do it!" Feather stormed.

Larry looked at Feather, then back at Jeremiah and Cody. Both nodded agreement.

"At the beginning of summer I would never have agreed to this." He took a deep breath and wiped the sweat from his forehead with the back of the terry cloth University of Indiana sweat band on his wrist. "But now . . . Feather, you're the only girl on the face of the earth I'd trust to do this."

"I know." She wrinkled her nose, launching a small armada of freckles. "I'm one of a kind."

"We've got to go out and get a bucket before we play defense," Larry reminded them. "If you have an open shot, take it, but be sure you're set and square to the basket."

Larry took the inbound pass and punched into the top of the key before bouncing it back out to Feather. Cody leaned into Freight Train under the basket in a scramble for best rebound position.

The quickness and speed of Feather's return pass

almost caught Larry off guard. It was more like a stagger than a planned move. As he spun, he leaped off the wrong foot and flung up a shot from the free-throw line.

The ball bounced off the glass and into the net.

"Bank!" Larry shouted. "Yes!"

The crowd roared.

"Lewis, you're the luckiest guy in Idaho!" Dink mumbled as he sprinted after the ball.

"Thank you. Thank you very much. I had a bowl of my lucky tapioca right before I came over!" Larry spouted as the Lewis and Clark Squad sprinted back to set up for defense.

"Remember the Feather-D!" Jeremiah shouted from the sidelines.

She and Larry quickly doubled-teamed Dink, who bounced the ball to Kenny McClain. Cody sprinted out to cover him, and the ball flew in to Freight Train.

He sported a wide I've-got-the-ball-and-we're-going-to-win grin on his round face. Then thin, long fingers with pink fingernails plucked the ball out of the air only inches from the Lions' dream of victory.

"Yes!" Jeremiah shouted, leading the cheers from the sidelines.

Feather instantly flung the ball out to Larry, who sailed it in to Cody. With his back to the basket, he faked right and went left with a little hook shot.

The ball bounced off the glass backboard high above the painted orange square . . . and missed the rim completely.

Freight Train, standing flat-footed and all alone, waited for the rebound.

"Hey, isn't that Bruce Baxter?" Feather shouted and waved her hand toward the far end of the gym.

"The actor in all those Magna-Cop movies?" Freight-Train Banks glanced over at the bleachers. The basketball rolled off his fingertips and into the key. Larry raced in to retrieve it and flung up an off-balance lay-in that sailed high above the rim and then dropped into the net without hitting the backboard.

"Yes . . . yes. We did it!" Larry hollered.

The crowd cheered.

The Lions stood stunned.

The Lewis and Clark Squad swarmed the sideline with high fives.

"I thought we lost it when Cody missed the hook shot," Jeremiah hollered above the buzz of noise from the bleachers.

"I should have made that. Great work, Feather!" Cody shouted. "I can't believe they fell for . . ." He looked around the bleachers. "Where's Feather?"

Larry pointed toward the main gym entrance to a crowd of people who seemed to include everyone else in the gym. "She's over there in the middle of that crowd talking to her good pal and buddy Bruce Baxter, I suppose."

"He's really here?" Cody choked. "No wonder it worked."

Larry slapped him on the back. "Either way we're in the semis. Two more games and we're summer league champs!"

"Two more wins," Jeremiah corrected.

"Same thing!" Larry bragged. "I wonder if Bruce Baxter wants my autograph?"

Cody could tell by Feather's face that she was totally bummed out. He sat on the concrete steps in front of the gym in the late August twilight and watched her plod across the half-filled gravel parking lot. From behind him the sounds of basketballs bouncing off polished wooden floors blended with shouts from enthusiastic parents and fans as the championship tournament continued.

The long black limousine crept out onto Halt's First Street. A trail of dust followed it out of town like the train on a bride's dress.

"Thanks for waiting, Cody," she called out before she got to him. "Where are Larry and Townie?"

"Oh, Larry's inside scouting our next opponent. He said we'll have practice tomorrow morning at ten. Townie went home to see if his mom had heard anything from his brothers. They're fighting that fire over in Montana. It blew up and hopped the fire break yesterday. He wanted to talk to her about it."

"Does he think they're in danger?"

"You know how he worries all the time. But they've been doing this for years. They're about the best in the business."

She plopped down next to Cody, pulled the rubber band off her ponytail, and let her hair cascade down over her shoulders. She balanced her elbows on her thin knees, her chin cradled in the palm of her hands. "Sometimes I wish I still had a brother to worry about," she spoke softly.

Cody stared out across the parking lot. *Lord, I never know what to say to Feather. Help her understand why her brother died.* He rubbed his upper arms with his hands and glanced up at her. "Well, Ms. Famous Actress, I can't believe Bruce Baxter came to town just to see you."

"Isn't that awesome? I seem to be a magnet for hand-some men." She raised her nose in the air for a moment and then lowered it. "Of course, he was on his way to Coeur d'Alene. He wanted to talk to me and couldn't find my phone number. I wish we had a phone. Maybe if I ever make some money, I'll pay for one myself."

Cody realized he was staring at her legs and quickly looked out toward First Street. "What did he want to talk to you about? Or is that personal?"

"It's no secret. It will be in all the tabloids by Monday. He said he broke up with Julia Margo and wanted to know if I was available."

Cody felt his stomach drop. "He what?"

"That's what I like about you, Cody Wayne Clark. You're the only boy in the entire world who would believe me. You can tell when I'm joking, can't you?"

"Oh, yeah." Cody hoped the evening shadows hid some of the blush on his face. "I knew that."

"Besides, you and me are a number. Dink Wilkins said that. It's all over town."

Cody cleared his throat and stared down at his worn Nikes that had once belonged to his brother Denver.

"Feather, I'm kind of, you know, slow about some things. Just exactly what does 'being a number' mean?"

She shook her head and grinned. "It means you can't hop in a jet and fly off to Las Vegas with Julia Margo."

"What?" Cody knew beyond a doubt that his face was as red as the setting sun.

"Being a number means everyone in town expects to see us together all the time and stuff like that."

"Stuff like what?"

"Forget it. Do you really want to know why Bruce Baxter wanted to talk to me?"

"Sure. Was it about that commercial you made with him at Eureka's ranch?"

"Sort of. It came out so good they want me to do another one with them."

"No kidding? That's wonderful!" Cody blurted out. "Oh, man, is this a good day, or what?"

Feather sat up, then dropped her chin to her chest. "It's not all that good."

Cody rubbed the back of his neck. It felt sticky with dried sweat. "What are you talking about?"

Feather's head bobbed back and forth as she talked. "They want to tape it tomorrow and the next day."

"You're kidding." Cody leaned back on the concrete step and stared up at the graying sky. "They want you in a commercial, and they just let you know about it the day before?"

"Well, they couldn't exactly call me, fax me, or talk to my agent. I wonder if I ought to have an agent? I wonder how a person gets an agent? Anyway, he needs me to be in Coeur d'Alene by noon tomorrow."

"Did you tell him we've got a tournament going on?"

"Yeah. He said I'd have to choose between fame and basketball."

Cody sat back up. "What are you going to do?"

"What do you think I ought to do?" she implored.

"I don't know, Feather. We need you on the team, but it's really an incredible opportunity. I just don't know what to tell you."

"What would you like me to do?"

"Me?" Cody gulped.

"You want me to stay and play on the team, right?"

"I didn't say that."

"But you were thinking that. I can tell."

"You can?"

"I can always tell what you're thinking!"

"Then you can tell I'm thinking you ought to talk this over with your mom."

"Maybe you could talk it over with the Lord for me."

"You can pray about it yourself, Feather."

"Oh, I know, but you and Him being such good friends . . . Anyway, you're right. I'd better go tell my mom. She ought to be finishing work about now. What am I going to do, Cody? It's all your fault."

"My fault?"

"Yeah, you insisted that I be in that first commercial. If you had been in it, it would be you having to make this decision. I'm used to having to choose between the best of two bad situations, not the best of two good ones."

Cody watched her run across the parking lot.

It was a noisy, late summer night.

Cheers from the gym.

Yearling cattle bawling for their mamas.

A car backfiring on First Street.

Kids laughing on the swings in the city park.

Mrs. Moorehouse practicing the organ with the church windows open.

And someone trying to use up the remnants of summer firecrackers down near the lake.

It was one of those rare days when a town of 900 sounds like a town of 9,000.

Yet Cody felt totally alone.

Back to the basket.

In the key.

Fake right.

Pivot on your left foot.

Bank a hook shot.

One bounce off the glass, and the ball dives through the net.

A perfect two. It was 44 out of 50.

Cody Clark dribbled the ball with his left hand and drew his right through his shaggy brown hair. *That's not bad. Especially if you're thirteen years old and would rather rodeo than shoot baskets.*

This is crazy, Lord.

Larry called the practice the most important one of the whole summer, and nobody's here. Maybe I got it wrong. It must have been some other time. Larry's not even home. I can't remember practicing basketball all by myself.

Cody trudged back through the scattered pines on the lot that separated his yard from Larry's. He shoved open the front door and let the basketball thump aimlessly across the living room carpet. He flung open the refrigerator door and stared. Nothing looked good. The air felt cool on his sweat-covered face.

Finally he reached behind a glass casserole dish half filled with tamale pie and pulled out a Mountain Dew. He popped open the wide-mouthed can and flopped down on an oak stool next to the kitchen counter.

This is weird, Lord. Really weird.

This has been the most exciting, adventurous, fast-moving summer in my entire life. But it's like it ended two days too soon. No one's here for practice. No one's at home. It's like something big happened, and everyone forgot to tell me. There's probably a good explanation for it all.

Cody took a deep swig of the soda and grabbed up the black cordless telephone. He punched in the familiar number and waited as the hard plastic phone blared away with a busy signal. He dropped the phone back into its cradle and took another swig of Mountain Dew. Then he looked at the can.

A 3!

On a scale of 1 to 10, this Dew's a 3.

Cody dialed Jeremiah's phone number again and found it still busy. "Come on, Townie, quit talking to DeVonne!" He stepped out on the front porch and stared over at the Lewis driveway.

Maybe this is a joke. Maybe they're hiding in the trees just waiting to see what I will do. Larry Bird Lewis never ever misses a basketball practice. Not even to play a practical joke. Especially with the semifinals tonight! This is crazy. This is worse than dreaming about being stuck in a dark tunnel.

This is real.

Cody wrote a note to his mother on the white message board and scurried out the back door. Mounted on his green and gray mountain bike, he pedaled down the gravel and dirt street that connected his house and Larry's with First Street.

He had every intention in the world of going to Jeremiah's house. But when he reached the corner of First and Joseph, he turned toward Feather's instead. He was almost to her house before he realized where he was headed. He pounded on the cracked and peeling white-painted screen door.

"Feather? Are you home?"

Maybe she's over at Larry's now. If she went down the alley, I could have missed seeing her. I'll just go on over to Townie's. Someone has to be there. The phone line's busy. This is a strange morning. If I'd known there was no practice, I could have gone to see Grandma and Grandpa with Mom and Denver.

Cody was surprised to find Rocky Hammers standing next to his bike when he went back out to the front of Feather's house. Cody looked up and down the street as he approached Rocky.

"You looking for J. J. and Devin?" Rocky asked.

"Eh, yeah, I guess. I don't think I've seen you all summer without the others around," Cody acknowledged.

Rocky nodded toward the house. "What about you, Clark? You all alone?"

Cody glanced back toward Feather's front door. *I ought to say, "My brothers are just around the corner ready to beat you to a pulp if you try anything."* He cleared his throat. "Yep, I'm alone. We were supposed—I mean, we're going to have some practice this morning. What about the Pirates? You guys practicing?"

"That's what I wanted to talk to you about." Rocky glanced down at the top of his black Nikes. "I quit the team."

"Really? Why?" Cody gasped. "You guys are really good."

"At street ball maybe. But the Squad has the flash. Everybody in Halt knows that."

"That's mainly Larry. I've got about as much flash as a grain truck. Why did you quit?"

"Cody, J. J. intends to get even with you. I'm tired of it."

"Get even for what? I thought everything was settled."

"Everyone in town has heard about him crawling across the Buy Rite parking lot when you helped catch that armed robber. He can't live with that."

"But I didn't really aim the gun at him. And I sure didn't make him crawl."

"He's planning on taking you down with an elbow or knee or head-butt during the championship game."

"We haven't even made it to the championship game," Cody reminded him.

"Everybody knows it's goin' to be the Squad and the Pirates. That's been obvious since the beginning of summer."

"But why did you quit, Rocky? You're probably the best player on the team. They can't make it to the championship with just two guys, no matter how rough they play."

"J. J.'s cousin Ty is coming in to play the last two games."

"Ty?" Cody gulped.

"Yeah. Remember, he was in school a few weeks before Christmas?"

"He got kicked out for punching Mr. Mills."

Rocky reached up and pushed his black hair out of his eyes. "Yeah, well, he is now a member of the Pirates."

"How can they do that? They can't add a member this late in the season, can they?"

"J. J. added his name to our team as a fourth member in July. I guess Ty was supposed to come up and spend the summer with him. But he never showed. Anyway, we've had him on our roster all the time. So when I told J. J. I was going to quit if he insisted on playing dirty, he said it didn't matter. He'd have Ty come up and finish the season."

"How about Devin?" Cody pressed.

"I think he's afraid to quit. He won't play too dirty, but he won't stand up to J. J.—that's for sure."

"So how come you came to talk to me, Rocky?"

"'Cause some things just aren't right. You know what I mean? This just isn't right. Of course, I don't know if there's anything you can do about it."

Cody sighed and reached down to pick up his bike. "Rocky, what would you do if you were me?"

"I'd make sure I didn't win the semis. That way you'll never have to face J. J. and Ty, and maybe they'd be so happy being champs again that they'd just ignore you." Rocky jammed his hands in his jeans pockets and started down the street. Then he turned back. "But I know you won't do that. You're a Clark, and everybody knows the Clarks don't back away from anything. I don't know what you're going to do about it, Cody. J. J.'s a jerk. Just don't get yourself hurt. Summer league's not that important."

"Thanks for the warning, Rocky."

"I didn't tell you anything. You understand?"

Cody studied Rocky's slumping shoulders as he back-walked down the street. "Yeah . . . I understand."

I understand I'd better go talk to Townie. This is getting crazier every day. Lord, I absolutely don't understand anything about J. J. I know You created him and that Jesus died for him, just like for all the rest of us. But I don't know why he has to act the way he does.

The fastest way from Feather's house to Jeremiah's was to swing down the alley behind the Buy Rite Market. Cody dropped his bike by the abandoned gas pump in front of the market and shoved open the green screen door.

The smell of teriyaki beef jerky greeted him as he approached the counter where a tall, strong, gray-haired man was waiting on a customer. "Mr. Addney, is Feather's mom working today?"

"Nope. They already left for Coeur D'Alene."

"They what?"

"You knew about that deal to make another commercial with Bruce Baxter, didn't you?"

"Well, yeah . . . but I thought . . ."

"Won't be back until late Monday night, I reckon. She didn't want Feather to miss the first day of school."

"Feather's going to school in Halt? She's not being home-schooled any longer?"

"How about that? I knew something about your girl-friend that you didn't."

Cody turned back to the door. *You know a whole bunch that I don't. I didn't think she'd go film that commercial without telling me. Sometimes it seems like we're really good friends, and sometimes it's like I don't know her at all.*

The ride to Jeremiah's house was downhill for a block, then level for two, and uphill for the final one. But the gravel streets of Halt seemed all uphill as Cody stood on the pedals and pumped his bike.

The clouds that had been scattered and white early in the day now hung low, dark, and heavy. There was a slight chill in the air. Cody recognized it as the annual north-central Idaho end-of-summer-and-school-is-about-to-start kind of chill.

At least, that's what he hoped it was.

Jeremiah Yellowboy sat on the front step of their blue and white single-story house when Cody coasted up to the front yard and dropped his bike on the gravel. He jogged toward the porch.

"Townie, am I glad to see you! This whole morning is totally weird. Hey, aren't we supposed to be having basketball practice? I was over there all by myself. Even Larry didn't show. I mean, his whole family's gone. I can't imagine anything keeping him away from practice. Anyway, it looks like it's just the three of us this weekend. Mr. Addney said Feather and her mom went up to Coeur D'Alene to film that commercial. Did she say anything to you about having made up her mind? She didn't say anything to me. We've been a team all year, and now we'll have to play the semis and the championship without her. Speaking of championship, did you hear that Rocky quit the Pirates? He told me . . . I mean, I heard that he quit, but J. J.'s having his cousin Ty take his place. Ty's the only guy I ever met that made J. J. seem normal. You know what I mean?"

Jeremiah's head slumped to his lap, and Cody stared at the top of the black butch haircut. Jeremiah pulled up the tail of his red Chicago Bulls tank top and wiped his eyes.

"Townie?" Cody's voice softened. "Are you crying?"

Two

✳

"*T*wo Ponies and Sweetwater?" Cody gasped.

Jeremiah continued to wipe his eyes as he nodded.

"Are they . . ." Cody couldn't even choke out the final word. Tears puddled in the corners of his eyes.

Jeremiah's voice was so low and soft Cody had to lean down to hear the words. "A life support helicopter flew them to the burn center in Denver. As far as the Forest Service spokesman knew, they were still alive . . . barely."

"Do you know what happened?"

"A firestorm trapped four of them in a canyon. They hardly had time to pull out their 'shake-and-bake' bags. The other two died."

Tears rolled down Cody's face as he thought about Jeremiah's older brothers. He flopped down on the step and used the hem of his black sleeveless T-shirt to wipe his face.

"Pray for them, Cody."

Cody tried to take a deep breath, but it felt shallow. *Lord, I don't know . . . I can't . . . what do I . . . this is so . . .*

"Please, Cody," Jeremiah choked.

"Lord Jesus, this is Cody. I've been praying a lot for me lately. Forget about that, Lord. This is important. I really pray that You'll keep Two Ponies and Sweetwater from dying. Lord, this just might be the most important prayer I ever prayed. In Jesus' name, amen."

"Amen," Jeremiah mumbled. "They just got to live, Cody. It would kill my mom if she lost them."

"How's she doing?"

"She's been on the phone for an hour trying to get an airline ticket to Denver."

"Are you going with her?"

"Yeah, if she can get two tickets. But she has to find someone to take care of the girls."

"I bet my mom would do it."

"She said no one's at home at your house."

"Oh, yeah. Mom and Denver are over at Grandpa's. Tell her to call over there."

Cody remained seated on the concrete steps while Jeremiah retreated into the house. Cody heard the phone ring inside.

Lord, I've been stewing around about a basketball game . . . and about J. J. That's not so important, is it? Townie's brothers—that's important. My mind's too small. Mostly I just think about me.

Jeremiah returned carrying two sodas. "You want a Dew?"

"I guess not. Thanks, anyway. I just had a lousy one."

"You ever notice that the quality of the soda improves

with how good your day's been going?" Jeremiah took a big gulp from the green aluminum can.

"In that case, you got a lousy Dew."

Jeremiah looked at the can. "Oh, it's a 5. Things have perked up a little. The hospital just called and said they were stabilized for now, whatever that means. Mom got me and her a ticket on a flight out of Lewiston at noon. I'm on standby, but they think it will work."

"That's great . . ." Cody stopped midsentence, and his head dropped. "Actually what I mean is, it's, eh, better."

"You guys will have to carry on without me." Jeremiah sat down next to Cody. "You can do it. Feather's a good player. What did you tell me about her?"

Cody leaned back on his elbows. "She's gone, Townie."

"She went to do that commercial? Did she tell you she was leaving?"

"Nope."

"Whoa . . . then just you and Larry were at practice?"

"Larry didn't show. His whole family's gone."

"Man, what's happening?" Jeremiah groaned. "It's like the Squad is coming apart right at the end of summer."

"You're telling me."

"Cody, I have to go with Mom."

"Townie, there is no basketball game on the face of the earth as important as your brothers."

"Yeah . . . I hope Larry feels the same way."

"If he doesn't, he needs to learn."

Neither boy spoke for a couple of minutes.

Finally Jeremiah cleared his throat. "Man, we had a good team this summer, didn't we?"

"Yep. I don't know if we'll ever have one that good again."

"It's kind of like God just put us all together on purpose, wasn't it?" Jeremiah offered.

"Yeah. That's what I was thinking."

"I wonder why He broke us up right before the championship?"

"Maybe we would have won and bragged too much."

"We could have beaten them," Jeremiah announced.

"The Pirates?"

"Yeah. I really think J. J., Rocky, and Devin were headed for a fall."

"Hey, that's why I came over here!" Cody sat up straight. "Rocky told me he quit the Pirates, and J. J.'s bringing in his cousin Ty to finish the tournament."

"Ty? I thought he was in juvenile detention down in Pocatello."

"I guess he's not there anymore."

"They bring him in just to beat us up?"

Cody shrugged. "Me mainly."

"J. J. still on your case?"

"Yeah, that's why Rocky quit."

Jeremiah chugged the last of the soda. "Maybe the Lord knows what He's doing."

"What do you mean?"

"Well, if it's down to Larry and you, we won't make the championship, and we won't have to worry about the Pirates."

"That's one way to look at it."

"Larry will probably want you two to play them."

"We have the semis tonight. We'll never get by the Porcupines."

"Cody, I'm really sorry. I feel like I'm letting you guys down."

"Townie, it's been a great summer. It might be a lousy fall, but it's been a great summer."

Jeremiah stood up. "I'd better go help my mom pack."

Cody shoved himself to his feet. He could feel tears in his eyes again. "If you want to, you could call me from Denver."

"You know I will. And thanks, cowboy."

"What for?"

"The prayer . . . and the tears."

"Well, go on. Get packed up before I start bawling like a girl."

"It's a good thing Feather didn't hear you say that."

Cody nodded and trudged to his bike.

He braked to a stop at the end of the Lewis driveway and stared at the empty garage. He rode on home and dropped his bike on the grass in the front yard. On his trip through the house, he paused only long enough to jam on his black cowboy hat and pluck up his coiled rope.

He crashed out the back door and parked himself about fifteen feet behind the plastic steer head mounted on a bale of straw. The loop whirled around his head, floated through the cool Idaho air, and dropped around the steer.

Lord, it feels like we've been racing around the track all summer, and we ran out of gas right before the finish line. Maybe it's time for school to start.

Cody continued the cycle of tossing the rope and unhooking the loop from the steer head.

I ought to go with Denver to the rodeo in Missoula and see Prescott and Reno. The Squad was too close. We each have our own lives to live. Important things to do. Critical things to do.

It was an extremely familiar sound.

Thump.

Thump.

Thump.

Cody couldn't remember when a basketball being dribbled on bare dirt sounded so good. He coiled his rope and sprinted to the side of the house in time to see Larry Lewis coming through the vacant lot that separated their houses.

"Larry! Where've you been?"

Blond hair bouncing in time with the basketball, Larry jogged up beside Cody. "You're not going to believe this!"

"What happened?"

"I was kidnapped!"

"By space aliens, right?"

"Nah. By my dad."

"How do you get kidnapped by your own dad?"

Larry waved his hand in the air. "He said, 'Get in the car or else!'"

"Or else what?"

"He didn't say. Mom and him needed me and Kevin to go to town with them. It was all some big secret, and I didn't think about calling you until we were halfway down the grade. Did practice go all right?"

Cody looped his coiled rope over his shoulder. "I had a good practice, but—"

"Great. I knew you guys could get along without me. For one practice anyway. This is totally incredible. You aren't going to believe what my parents did."

"They sold Kevin?"

Larry paused and then broke into a grin. "Just the opposite. What could be the worst thing that could possibly happen in my family?"

"They cloned Kevin?" Cody teased.

"Almost. We go down to Lewiston, and I have to keep an eye on Kev while Dad takes Mom to the doctor. When they're through, they take us out to a late breakfast at Waffles-by-the-Stack."

"So what did happen to your family?"

"It's not what happened but what's going to happen in about six months," Larry moaned.

"Are you guys moving back to Indiana?"

"No, you dunce. My mother's going to have a baby," Larry blurted out.

"You're joking!" Cody choked.

Larry rolled his eyes as he bounced the ball on the dirt. "Why on earth would I joke about that?"

"But . . . isn't she . . ."

"Too old? That's exactly what I told her. I think my exact words were, 'Mother, how could you do this to me?' This is the most humiliating thing that ever happened in my life! My own mother, pregnant! What do we need another kid for anyway? They have me and Kevin. What more could parents want?"

"Maybe they want a daughter?"

"Why?"

"Well," Cody stammered, "you know . . . it's sort of a mother thing to want a daughter."

"It's disgusting, if you ask me," Larry fumed. "No one inquired if I wanted a sister."

"I suppose they figured it was their decision."

"Well, they blew it this time. Pretty soon she'll be fat as a toad. That will be humiliating. Maybe she'll stay indoors, and no one will see her."

Cody scratched his shaggy brown head. "Maybe it won't be all that bad."

"Hah! You're the youngest in your family. I still have nightmares about when Kevin was born."

"For most families, having another child is good news."

"That's what my dad said. Well, at least nothing will happen this weekend." He began to spin the basketball on his finger. "You said you three had a good practice?"

"No, I said *I* had a good practice. I was the only one there."

Larry whirled around. "What do you mean?"

"Mr. Addney said Feather took off with her mom to tape that television commercial with Bruce Baxter."

"It's down to you, me, and Townie?"

"Oh no, it's worse than that."

Larry caught the ball and held it.

Cody took a deep breath. "Two Ponies and Sweetwater

got burned really bad in the Montana forest fire. Townie and his mother are flying to Denver today."

"We've got a semi and the championship!"

"It's down to you and me, partner."

"But we can't play them with only two."

"Maybe we should just drop out."

"Quit? I can't quit."

"It would be better than you and me getting humiliated in the semis. All summer long different teams were short-handed from time to time due to vacations and stuff. So they forfeited. Now maybe it's our turn."

"The word *forfeit* does not exist in my vocabulary!" Larry fumed. "This is the championship tournament. No! It can't be. This is what we worked hard for all summer. This is payday. We can't back out now. Has Townie left yet?"

"I don't know. If he hasn't, he will be in the next few minutes."

"Come on. If we use our bikes, maybe we can catch him."

"And what then? Lay a guilt trip on him and try to force him to change his mind? Not me. I won't do that." Cody grabbed Larry by the shoulder. "Let it go, Larry. There really are some things more important than a basketball game."

Larry tossed the basketball to the ground and then sat on it. He wiped his nose with the back of his hands. He rubbed his eyes on the sleeves of his University of Indiana T-shirt.

Cody plopped down in the grass and dirt next to him

and fingered the coiled rope in his hand. *Lord, I know this tournament means more to Larry than to any other kid in town. All of a sudden the summer seems so individual. It's not the Squad anymore; it's four kids—each with their own needs and agenda. Except for me. What's my agenda? Stay out of trouble and keep out of the spotlight. So far this summer I haven't done very well with that.*

Larry drew x's and o's in the dirt. "You're right, cowboy. I get so caught up with basketball I forget other things. Are Townie's brothers going to die?"

"They don't know. That's why they have to hurry to the burn center in Denver."

Larry stared out through the pine trees. "Cody, did you ever have someone in your family die?"

"Not really. My grandpa's brother died a couple of years ago, but he was kind of an old hermit. I didn't know him very well. How about you?"

"My grandpa died last year. My mom's dad."

"Did he live close to you guys?"

"In our living room."

"What?"

"He had cancer, and he stayed with us the last six months or so. The final six weeks Mom and Dad rented a hospital bed and put it right in the living room."

"That must have been rough, watching someone die that close."

"We played cribbage almost every day."

"He felt good enough to play cribbage?"

"Kevin would hold the cards for him, and he'd tell him

which ones to play." Larry rubbed his eyes on his sleeve again. "I learned a lot those last six weeks."

"About cribbage?" Cody asked.

"About everything."

Larry went back to drawing x's and o's in the dirt with his finger. Cody lay back in the grass and stared at the clouds that were starting to stack up over the Bitterroot Mountains in the east. *Lord, I've been with Larry all summer, and I never once heard him talk about this. People are complex. Just when I think I have them all figured out, they break out of the mold.*

I thought I knew everything about Larry.

I thought I knew everything about Feather. Why didn't she tell me she was leaving?

"Cody, what really happens when people die?"

"If they believe in Jesus, they go to heaven."

"I know that. But how does that work?" Larry probed.

"I don't know all the details. We studied it in Sunday school last year, but I don't remember everything. I think the Bible says we are never separated from the Lord. So I guess when our bodies die, we go right then to be with Him."

"You know what my grandpa said before he died?"

"Did he die right there in the living room? You were there?" Cody quizzed.

"Yeah, we were all there."

"What did he say?" Cody asked.

Larry turned away and wiped his eyes. "For the first time in two weeks, Grandpa smiled. Then he said in a really clear voice, 'Well, isn't that nice!'"

"Then he died?"

"Yep."

"You figure he saw something?"

"Yeah, but what do you suppose it was?"

"Maybe it was Jesus coming to get him."

Larry nodded his head. "That would be nice, wouldn't it?"

The tops of the pine trees swayed left and right as the storm clouds continued to stack tight. The sixty- to ninety-foot Ponderosas pointed like green fingers trying to grab onto a cloud. It was transition weather—the kind of day that says to put up your summer clothes and pull out some warmer ones.

Larry's words were so soft Cody could barely hear them. "What about those who don't believe? Where do they go?"

Cody laid his bare arm over his eyes and focused on total blackness. "The Bible says they all end up in a place called hell."

Larry cleared his voice and took a deep breath. "I say . . . we take them on—and go down swinging!"

"Who?"

"The Porcupines."

"Just you and me?"

"Why not? It's legal, isn't it?"

"Yeah, but what chance do the two of us have against three? All they have to do is spread it out, and they have a man in the clear all the time."

"Who knows? Maybe someone will twist an ankle on the first play, and they will have to play with two."

"It could be humiliating," Cody insisted.

"So could forfeiting. At least, we could give it our best shot."

"Larry, are you sure your dad would let us play with only two?"

"He let them do it all summer. Why not in the tournament? But I'll check with him. What do you say, cowboy?"

"It sounds totally weird even to try it."

"Just the kind of thing you'd expect from the Lewis and Clark Squad?"

A wide grin broke across Cody's face. "Yeah, I'll do it."

"All right! There's always a chance. But we better develop some two-on-three plays."

"Maybe we should go over to your house and shoot some hoops."

"First, I've got to work out a game plan," Larry insisted. "Then we need to go out to your ranch and practice at the barn."

"Why?"

"I don't want anyone in town to know that we are only going to have two players. The element of surprise could be worth four points."

"We live on a dead-end street. No one comes up here anyway."

"We can't take any chances. Let's go out to the barn at 1:00. I'll have everything all figured out by then."

Cody pulled himself to his feet and brushed off his Wranglers.

Larry dribbled the ball on the grass. "You know, this might be our last practice."

Cody shoved his hat back on his head. "Yeah, it will seem funny not to have Townie and Feather."

"When does junior high basketball practice start?"

"Around the first of November."

"Maybe I could talk my dad into organizing an after-school fall league. Would that be cool, or what?"

"It would be nice to keep the Squad together," Cody agreed.

"Oh, wow!" Larry stopped dribbling and clutched the ball under his arm. "I just thought of our opening defensive play. Whoa! I better go write this down. We can do it, Cody! I think we can beat them!"

Cody stared after Larry as he ran through the trees toward his house. *Lord, I've never known anyone like Larry. Always upbeat, always enthusiastic. I like having him for a friend. Even if his mind is consumed with basketball.*

At 12:15 Cody thought about calling his grandparents to see if his mom and Denver were still there.

At 12:30 he made himself an extra-sharp cheddar cheese sandwich with yellow mustard and dill pickle on sourdough bread. He washed it down with the dregs of some pink lemonade he found in the back of the refrigerator. At least he thought it was lemonade. It had a slight pear juice taste to it.

At 12:45 he wrote a note on the message board explaining that he and Larry had ridden their bikes to the ranch to practice.

The dryland pasture on the Clark ranch was turning brown, just waiting for the first frost of autumn to complete the life cycle. Mornings were already dipping into the upper 30s. Cody knew summer weather would not last much longer.

County Line Road still held the moisture of a rain two days earlier. There was no dust at all from the rigs that passed Cody and Larry as they biked out to the ranch. The heavy, dark clouds in the sky held evaporation to a minimum as Cody led the way.

Most of the conversation concerned Rocky Hammers quitting the Pirates and the outside possibility of facing an angry J. J. and an unpredictable Ty in a championship game.

When they turned off the gravel road onto the dirt one, Larry nodded toward the clouds looming above the treetops. "Hey, you think it's going to rain?"

"Maybe it will hold off until tonight."

"Or until after practice. I have ten awesome plays. If they all work, we'll have 20 points."

"And if they don't work?"

"We'll just hope the electricity goes off, and they have to postpone the tournament. Anyway, I figure if we're on our game, we can make some points. It's defense that will be difficult."

"Maybe we could ask the Porcupines to have two of them stand next to each other and make it easier for us to guard them," Cody laughed.

"One of our plays is just like that."

"Just like what?"

Larry stood up and pedaled. "Instead of spreading out and letting them double-team one of us, we bunch up in one play. They'll guard us three-on-two, but we'll break to the corners, and they'll have a split second to decide who guards whom. A window of opportunity."

"That will only work once."

"That's all we need, partner." Larry sped ahead of Cody. "I figure if we work the plays, shoot 90 percent or better, and have a couple lucky breaks, we could keep the game close."

"And if not?"

"We get to spend the rest of the weekend down at the Buy Rite playing Cool Rig."

They coasted past the corrals and up to the huge fading red barn.

"Hey, do you need to feed Eureka's horses?" Larry asked.

"Nope. I fed them this morning. This is my second bike ride to the ranch today."

"Nothing ever changes out here," Larry remarked. "It looks exactly the same as it did six weeks ago."

"It looks exactly the same as it did six years ago," Cody laughed. "The paint was peeling off then, too." He propped his bike against the barn door. "We'd better get started. I really do think it's going to rain."

"Okay." Larry pulled a stack of folded papers from his back pocket. "Which do you want to go over first—our defense plays or our offensive ones?"

Cody shook his head and grinned. "When in the world did you have time to do all of that?"

"I ate my lunch in my room for one thing. But a lot of the plays I had in my files."

"Your files?"

"When I wake up in the night and can't get back to sleep, I think up plays. So I write them down and file them."

"Two-on-three plays?"

"Hey, I've got everything. You ought to see my one-on-five plays."

"You've got to be kidding!"

"Well, they only work if the five are in kindergarten."

The dirt around the barn was moist enough to keep the dust down and yet not stick to the ball. Larry insisted that they run through each play five times. It started to sprinkle when they were on Semifinal #8—Offense. And the clouds opened up and roared when they got to Semifinal #9—Defense.

"Let's wait this thing out in the barn," Cody hollered.

"We're not through."

"We're getting soaked. Grab your bike. I'll chase down the ball."

Larry sprinted to the bikes as Cody scooped up the basketball and trotted to the barn door. By the time he got inside the dark barn, his sleeveless black T-shirt was soaking wet.

Larry stood at the doorway. "It's really pouring!"

"It's cold! Close the door," Cody commanded.

Both boys huddled in the shadowy darkness of the barn.

"What do we do now?"

"Wait it out. It won't last all afternoon," Cody advised. "Let's go into the tack room and build a fire in the wood-stove. We can at least dry off our clothes."

Larry didn't move. "I didn't know you guys raised pigs."

"Pigs? We don't have any pigs."

"Well, there's one right over there!" Larry pointed to a stall.

"I don't see any . . ."

"I never knew pigs had tusks! What breed is that?"

"Tusks! Where?"

"Over there. . . . Wow, here he comes!" Larry yelled.

"Up the ladder," Cody hollered. "Get up that loft ladder." He almost shoved Larry up ahead of him. "That's no pig. It's a javelina!"

The three-foot-long, dark gray animal with a white band across its chest charged right at the base of the ladder.

"Is it barking?" Larry panted when he reached the loft.

"Sort of."

"What's that rattling sound?"

"They do that with their teeth."

"I take it he's ticked off at us."

"She."

"You can tell it's a she in the darkness?"

"It's Harriet."

"Harriet the javelina? You know all the wild hogs by name?"

"She's not a wild hog. She's a peccary."

"How come I never heard of them?" Larry gasped. "All

the tramping around in the woods we've done, and no one ever warned me about wild . . . javelinas."

The nearly tailless fifty-pound animal continued to circle the base of the ladder, small ears erect and spearlike teeth rattling.

"Harriet's the only one around here," Cody explained. "When ol' Mase Montgomery quit the Sixes Ranch in Texas and moved to that cabin west of town, he brought two tame javelinas with him. Well, the first day in Idaho, Harriet ran off into the woods and has lived off the land ever since."

"When was that?" Larry asked.

"About five years ago."

"What about the other one?"

"Harry?"

"Yeah, is he still at that man's cabin?"

"Nope," Cody replied. "He got run over by the propane truck. Harriet still roams the hills. Only she usually doesn't head for the barn until it snows."

"How do we get her away from the base of the ladder? Wait until she goes out of the barn on her own?"

"We shut the doors, so we can't chase her out. Besides, she won't back down from anything."

"Oh, great! I'm starting to get really cold. I don't suppose you have a woodstove in the hay loft?"

"Nope, but we can bury ourselves in the straw," Cody suggested.

"You're kidding, right?"

"You'd rather sit there and freeze?"

"Why don't we drop a bale of hay or something on it."

"We don't want to injure her."

"Why not? She certainly wants to injure us."

"Harriet's kind of like an adopted wild pet around Halt. Everyone looks out for her."

"But she's mean and ugly."

"And she has a nasty bite. She bit Mr. Kline, a horse buyer from Yakima, one time."

"What happened?"

"She lived."

"What happened to the horse buyer, Clark!"

"He quit coming over here." Cody dove into a pile of loose straw. "Come on, L. B., we can get out of the cold air this way. She'll settle down after a while, and we can sneak out."

"And ride home in the rain?"

"Welcome to an Idaho autumn."

"But it's not even September!"

"That's why I said Idaho autumn, not Idaho winter," Cody jibed.

Three

✧

*T*he crash of thunder seemed to center only inches above the red barn. It rattled each piece of the sheet-metal roof. Both Cody and Larry exploded out of the straw to their feet.

"That was close!" Larry gasped.

Cody peeked out the loft door at the shadows in the pasture. "How long were we asleep?"

Larry glanced down the loft ladder. "I don't know. Man, I can't believe it. That javelina is sleeping at the foot of the ladder and didn't even wake up. Maybe it's dead."

"Why don't you go down there and kick her to make sure," Cody teased.

Larry sauntered over next to Cody. "What are we going to do?"

Cody pushed the loft doors completely open. "Let's climb down the ropes, then sneak back in, and get our bikes."

"And ride home in the rain?"

"Sounds better than staying here," Cody maintained.

Larry glanced down at the dirt yard where puddles had

now formed. He pointed at the ropes and pulley. "I've never used one of these before."

"Piece of cake, Lewis. I'll let you down. Then you let me down," Cody announced.

Cody eased the white-knuckled Larry Lewis down into the rain and mud. Then he tossed the basketball to him and grabbed the rope. "You ready?" Cody called.

Larry flashed him a thumbs-up sign.

Cody swung away from the loft door. The jar of his full weight on the one-inch hemp rope lifted Larry off the ground. Cody descended about two feet as Larry continued to rise. Suddenly Larry turned loose of the rope and dropped back to the mud.

"No!" Cody hollered. He clung to the rope but crashed into the muddy yard. He flung off the rope just as he hit and tried to roll toward the barn door. He ended up in the middle of the biggest mud puddle on the ranch. He sat straight up and washed the mud off his hands in the ice-cold puddle water.

"I'm sorry!" Larry wailed, and he ran to Cody's side. "I told you I didn't know how to operate one of those."

Cody struggled to his feet. His Wrangler jeans were heavy with mud and water. "Well, it was—exciting!" Cody tried to brush his wet hair out of his eyes and succeeded in smearing mud across his forehead. "Let's get our bikes and go home before something really serious happens to us."

Larry swallowed hard. "You want me to go in there and pull out our bikes?"

"Let's go together. If we wake up Harriet, we'll just hop on the bikes and pedal as fast as we can."

"How fast can javelinas run?" Larry asked.

"Let's not find out. But if that thunder didn't wake her, we should be all right."

Cody and Larry sloshed their way to the barn door. The old door moaned pitifully as Cody cracked it open a couple of inches.

"Can you see Harriet?" Larry asked, from behind Cody.

"No, it's too dark. But I can see the bikes, and she's not around them. Let's run for them. The last one out kicks the door closed."

"Can you see her over there?"

Cody wiped the rainwater off his eyebrows and his nose. "No. Can you?"

"I can't see anything."

Cody slowly swung the wide door until it stood open about two feet. "Okay, L. B. Let's go!"

The soaking wet jeans rubbed on Cody's thighs as he sprinted across the dry dirt floor. He grabbed the cold handlebars, threw himself on the bike, and pedaled out the door into the storm. A frenzied yap and rattle of teeth caused him to look back over his shoulder. A panicked Larry Bird Lewis rode out the barn door.

"Kick the door shut, Larry!" Cody screamed into the cascading rainstorm.

Larry shot straight out into the yard and pedaled as fast as he could, his basketball tucked under his left arm. A hairy creature with lowered tusks flew out behind him and nipped at Larry's rear tire.

"Don't let her bite your tire!" Cody screamed as he continued to pedal furiously out of the yard to the muddy road that led down the sloping pasture land.

"Clark, wait for me! Don't leave me back here with this hog from Hades!" Larry screamed.

"Keep your speed up!" Cody called. "I think she's getting tired."

"She's getting tired? I'm getting tired!"

When they passed Eureka Blaine's driveway, the javelina was only two feet behind Larry's rear tire.

When they reached the mud and gravel of County Line Road, Harriet was no more than one foot behind him.

"I can't do it, Cody. She's going to catch me," Larry screamed.

"Pump it, Lewis! She can't run all the way back to town!" Cody hollered back.

"I can't go any faster."

"Go to the other side. Maybe she'll chase me!"

With mud flying off the rear tire and splattering his face, Cody looked back as Larry switched to the left side of County Line Road. The little javelina, with legs whirling, switched sides without losing ground.

"Cody, do something, or a brilliant NBA career is about to be hog food!" Larry cried.

"Bomb her!"

"What?"

"Bomb her with the basketball!" Cody hollered.

"My good basketball?"

"You told me it's the worst one you have, and you're tossing it at the end of summer."

"Yeah, but—"

"Summer's over, Lewis!"

The round Spalding sphere dropped silently out of the storm-slick hands of Larry Lewis. Like an intruder from outer space, it collided with the musky smelling, wet backside of Harriet the Javelina.

To the delight of both human observers, the infuriated peccary turned her wrath to the object only half her size. The basketball bounded off the roadway and fled under the lower strand of a rusted barbed-wire fence.

When they reached the crest of the hill right before the city limit sign, Cody and Larry paused to catch their breath.

"I can't believe I abandoned my basketball to that monster!" Larry moaned as he gasped for air.

"I can't believe we made it to town so fast. I've never pumped so hard in my life."

"She went under the fence. What's she doing with my ball?"

"Looks like she's going to roll it with her nose all over that pasture."

"She won't spike it or bite it, will she?" Larry asked.

"There's no way she can ever get her mouth around it," Cody replied. "We can probably ride out here tomorrow and pick it up."

"You can ride out here tomorrow. I'm sticking to town from now on. That's one crazy hog."

A slight explosion, like a balloon pop in a rainstorm, caused both boys to stare back down at the pasture.

"Well, that answers the question about whether she can spike it."

"My basketball!" Larry moaned.

"She saw it as an enemy."

"What's she doing with it now?"

"Looks like she's dragging it off to the forest in triumph." Cody began to chuckle and then tried to hold it back.

"What's so funny, Clark?"

"Look at us, Larry! We're soaking wet, covered with mud. We've biked three miles at top speed through a rainstorm with a fifty-pound wild hog chasing us."

"A javelina," Larry corrected.

"If we saw this scene in a movie, we'd be laughing our heads off."

"That's because if we saw it in a movie, it would be happening to someone else!"

"You have to admit it's funny!"

Larry's slow grin revealed his straight white teeth, the only thing left on him that was still white. "I'm just glad no one saw us."

"I don't know," Cody teased as they pedaled on into town, "if we had a video of it, we could make a fortune on one of those funny animal video shows. What do you say, Larry? Shall we do it again and shoot it for the contest?"

"You're out of your mind, Clark. I do not ever, and I repeat, ever, want to see another javelina as long as I live! Have I made myself clear?"

"It's tough to turn down such a money-maker. I think we could call it 'Larry's Lucky Bounce.'"

"This is not funny, Clark!"

"Sorry about your basketball, Larry. Maybe we can come out tomorrow and hunt for the remains to bury."

"I said, this isn't funny."

"Larry, my whole day has been uptight so far. Let me laugh a little. Don't you see anything funny about this?"

"You're covered with mud from head to toe—that's funny."

"Me? How about you?"

Larry pedaled a little faster and caught up with Cody. "And when you came crashing out of the loft and hit that big mud puddle, I thought I was going to explode trying to hold back from laughing."

"There wasn't anything funny about that," Cody snapped. "I could have broken my leg."

"I don't know. You were soaking wet, covered with mud, sitting in a downpour, trying to wash your hands in muddy water. That was funny!"

"I fail to see the humor."

"You're the one who told me to laugh."

"I meant . . . I meant . . ."

"You meant, laugh at me—not laugh at you," Larry prodded.

Suddenly both boys began to howl.

Cody caught his breath. "You're right, Larry. Now that we've lived through it, it was about the funniest sight I've seen in my life!"

"Well, Cody Wayne Clark, you just survived the attack of the killer javelina. Where are you going now?"

Cody flashed a phony smile. "I'm going to . . . to take a hot shower!"

"I think I'll get my mom to make me a bowl of my lucky popcorn," Larry announced as both boys turned up Camas

Street. "We've got the early game at 6:00 P.M. What time do you want to show up?"

"How about 5:58?" Cody suggested.

"You're kidding, right?"

"Why not? We had a good practice. We're both cold and tired—and we want to keep them guessing. If we show up early, they'll figure out quickly that there's only two of us, right?"

Larry shook his blond hair, and water sprayed all over his arms. "I like the way you think, Captain Clark."

Cody used the shower in the laundry room downstairs and emerged thoroughly clean and mostly warm. He found his brother Denver rummaging in the refrigerator.

"Hey, where's Mom?" Cody asked.

"She took the girls over to their house to gather up some clothes."

"Townie's sisters?"

"Yeah. They stayed at Mrs. Hightower's until we got back from Grandpa's."

"You hear about Two Ponies and Sweetwater?"

"Yeah. It doesn't sound good, does it, Cody Wayne?"

"You know what I've been thinking?" Cody quizzed.

Denver pulled out a block of Swiss cheese and broke off a corner. "You've been thinking what it would be like to get a phone call from a hospital in Arizona or Alberta and have them tell us that Prescott and Reno were in an accident and not expected to live."

Cody felt his chin drop. "How did you know that?"

"'Cause that, little brother, is exactly what I've been thinking since I heard about it."

"You too?"

"Yeah. It's scary, isn't it?"

"When are you leaving for Missoula?"

"As soon as I pack up. They entered me, so I'll have to go. Not many rodeos that have ever seen three Clark brothers."

"You think there will ever be a rodeo that has all four Clark brothers?"

"Come on with me," Denver urged. "Maybe they have a junior division."

"I wish I could. But I've got a basketball game tonight. It's just me and Larry now. Feather took off and didn't say anything to anyone."

"What do you mean, she didn't say anything? You read her letter, didn't you?"

Cody glanced around. "What letter?"

"Over there on the counter. She came by this morning while you were out feeding Eureka's horses. I left her note right where you'd see it."

Cody scampered to the counter and began to search. "Denver, there's no note over here!"

Denver waved his hand toward the far end next to the wall. "Over there, under your gloves."

Cody retrieved the pale pink envelope. "Under my gloves? You mean, I came in and tossed my gloves down on top of the letter?"

"Apparently."

"What's it say?" Cody asked.

"Little bro, I'll make a deal with you. You promise never to read any letter a girl writes to me, and I'll never read a letter a girl writes to you. Is it a deal?"

"Eh, yeah."

"Good. Now I'm going to pack up."

Even though the kitchen and living room were empty, Cody toted the letter outside to the wooden swing on the front porch. The rain had stopped, but the afternoon air felt cold on his arms. It would be daylight for several more hours, but the dark threatening clouds reduced visibility, and Cody switched on the front porch light.

He collapsed into the west end of the swing and used his finger for a letter opener. Across the top of the otherwise neat letter were the words, "Sorry I missed seeing you this morning, Cody." The rest of the letter was scrolled with Feather's perfect penmanship.

Dear Cody Wayne,

I decided to go to Coeur d'Alene today and check out this deal with the commercial. I didn't sleep much last night. You once told me I should do the things I'd regret not doing. Well, I know I'd regret it if I turned this down.

The only problem is, you didn't tell me that I might have a conflict with two things I must do at the same time. I decided on the commercial because I know what a great team you, Larry, and Townie make. It's been a privilege to be on the Squad this summer. I am confident you three can beat anyone in town. (Yes, even the Pirates!)

You guys have made my summer the best twelve weeks of my entire life. And you, Cody Wayne, have made me throw out almost everything I used to believe and accept a whole new basis for living my life.

Please don't get mad at me for running after this dream. If I get a chance, I'll call you from Coeur d'Alene.

Pray for me, Cody.

> *Forever yours,*
> *Feather*

P.S. Mom says if I make over $300 this weekend, I can get a phone installed. Is that cool, or what? It will be our first phone!

Forever yours? Is that the way she signs all her letters? Forever mine? What does that mean?

Alena Yellowboy was the first of Jeremiah's sisters to burst through the front door. She was followed by Brooke, Carley, and Danielle. At least, Cody thought that was the order.

Each had her waist-length black hair pulled straight back in a thick single braid. Each had dark brown eyes that danced. Each had round, permanently tanned faces. Each sported infectious smiles. In their jeans shorts, thongs, and T-shirts, they stair-stepped down from ten to six years old.

"Hi, Cody!" Danielle called out. "We get to stay at your house tonight!"

"That's what I heard. I'm glad you came over."

"See," eight-year-old Brooke blurted out, "I told you Cody likes me!"

"I, eh, like all of you," he stammered.

"Yes, but you like me the most, don't you?" Brooke pressed.

"I like you all the same," Cody tried to explain.

"He's just too bashful to admit it." Brooke shrugged.

"But I just—" Cody broke off when his mother walked into the house.

"Girls," Mrs. Clark cautioned, "you've given Cody an impossible task. You're all cute, talented, and charming. You can't possibly think a boy like Cody would be able to choose one over another."

Alena sighed. "She's right, you know. Cody's not used to being surrounded by beautiful women."

Cody glanced at Alena as she raised her thick, black eyebrows. *Beautiful women?*

"Where's your stereo?" Alena prodded. "Can I listen to your CDs?"

"It's in my—," Cody began.

"Where's your computer?" Brooke pressed. "Are you hooked to the Internet? I want to see if I have any E-mail."

Cody shook his head. "You get E-mail?"

"Where's your refrigerator?" Carley whined. "I'm hungry."

"Ask Mom about—"

"Where's your bathroom?" Danielle piped up. "I need to go potty."

"Mom!" Cody moaned. "This is all yours. I'm going to my room."

"I'll go with you!" Brooke insisted.

Margaret Clark blocked the path to the hall after Cody's retreat. "I need to get you girls settled downstairs first. Two will be in Prescott's room and two in Reno's. How do you want to pair off?"

Cody stood at his doorway and watched his mother herd the girls. She looked back up at him and winked.

Now there is one of the truly great mothers of all time. Lord, I drawed good, didn't I? Thank You.

His room was half dark due to the stormy afternoon sky. With legs still aching from the frantic bike ride home, Cody flopped on his back on top of his blue quilted bedspread and closed his eyes.

Rolly's ears stood at attention as Cody trotted the buckskin into the arena. The crowd cheered as he rode his horse up beside Denver, Reno, and Prescott.

"Here they are, folks, the Clark brothers from Halt, Idaho. Give them a big Cheyenne welcome 'cause we're seein' history in the making this afternoon."

Cody left one nylon pigging string coiled in his belt. He pulled the other out and clamped it in his teeth. He walked Rolly around outside the box, built a loop with his rope, twirled it over his head, and then placed the loop under his right arm and clamped it to his upper body.

"Give us a time to beat, little brother!" Denver called out.

"But not too fast," Reno teased. "We don't intend to give you first-place money like we did in Greeley."

Cody felt good about his brothers' ribbing but couldn't remember anything about Greeley, Colorado. *Why can't I remember any other rodeos?*

Rolly backed easily into the corner of the box, and Cody waited as the chute boss strung the barrier string. With a tug of the right hand, Cody jerked the front brim of his black Resistol cowboy hat down tight. Then he took the rope from under his arm and shook it out.

Rolly pranced and glanced at the massive bleachers crammed with screaming fans. Cody pushed the horse's head back to the chute where a white-faced Hereford calf stood waiting his turn to sprint across the Wyoming dirt. The calf tried to look back and see Cody, as if it knew nothing would start until Cody nodded his head.

A deep voice boomed, "Straighten him up, boys." Cody was shocked to discover it was his own voice.

At the sound of those words, Rolly stepped forward, and Cody reined him back. "I've got to re-set him, boys," Cody blurted out.

He walked Rolly to the front of the box and spun him around to the right. Then with a couple of light tugs on the reins, Cody backed him into the corner of the box. Rolly snorted and tugged at the bit.

"Whoa, boy . . . just a minute. We'll get him first lick, and you keep the rope taut."

Finally the calf turned his head and gazed off at the far end of the arena.

Cody nodded his head.

The chute gate crashed open, and at the same moment Cody touched his spurs lightly to Rolly's side.

The house galloped.

The barrier string flipped open.

The nylon loop whirled.

The crowd cheered.

Cody's full weight was on his right stirrup even as the loop settled around the calf's neck. Rolly reined up.

That was quick. Now if I can flank him fast, and if he doesn't kick . . .

When Cody's battered Justin Roper boots hit the loose dirt of the Frontier Days arena, he was already running toward the tethered calf. Calculating the best angle for tossing the animal to the ground, he ducked under the rope that Rolly kept taut.

Come on, baby . . . come to Cody. We're going to win some big money here today!

Cody's right palm burned a little as he slid his hand down the rope. Then within two steps of the animal, Cody stopped in his tracks.

The animal was suddenly gray, not red, and almost tailless, with little erect ears, a long snout, plus spearlike upper teeth, and protruding lower tusks gracing its sadistic smile.

A 260-pound javelina! I've got to flank and tie a javelina?

Suddenly the entire crowd grew quiet, and the musky-smelling peccary turned and charged at Cody.

Far off in the distance he could hear the haunting sounds of George Strait singing something about still having time to make a rodeo in Cheyenne . . .

The acoustic ceiling in his bedroom reminded Cody of a Martian landscape. George Strait continued to sing in the distance. But the distance was now only four feet to his stereo speakers.

I don't remember turning on the . . .

Cody sat straight up and stared into the smiling faces of Alena and Brooke Yellowboy. "What are you doing here?" he croaked.

"Watching you," Brooke announced.

"But—but I was asleep!"

Alena nodded her head. "We know. That's why we had the stereo turned down low."

"Did you know you sleep with your mouth wide open?" Brooke informed him.

"I what?" Cody felt his face flush.

"And your hands get sweaty." Brooke grimaced.

"Mom!" Cody called.

"She told us to come wake you up."

"She did?"

"Yes, she said you'd show us how to play Micro-Streetracer."

"On Nintendo?"

Alena turned to Brooke and giggled. "He's very bright, isn't he?"

All four girls huddled around the television set as Cody plugged in both controllers and started up the video game. "I didn't know girls liked to play games like this."

"We don't know if we like it or not. We've never tried it," Alena informed him.

"Jeremiah thinks it's the coolest video game on the

face of the earth," Danielle rattled on from her sprawled position on the couch.

"Well, there you go, ladies. Have fun." Cody wandered off to the kitchen. His mother was burying cooked bacon and cold Monterey Jack cheese in the middle of raw meat loaf.

"Thanks for getting the girls situated, Cody."

"How long do you think they'll stay with us?"

"I just talked to Carmen, and she said her sister Lucy will come pick them up tomorrow afternoon."

"You talked to Mrs. Yellowboy? Is she in Denver already?"

Cody's mom held her finger to her lips and whispered, "Shhh. The girls don't know much yet. Carmen doesn't want them to get upset any sooner than necessary. She and Jeremiah were at the airport in Salt Lake City waiting for a flight out. I guess most of the flights are overbooked, being the end of summer and the last chance to get away before school starts."

Cody leaned close and whispered, "What has she heard? How are Two Ponies and Sweetwater?"

"Still in stable condition. They say the next forty-eight hours are the most crucial."

"It scares me, Mom."

"They're in the Lord's hands, Cody Wayne. There's nothing we can do but trust Him."

"I know that, but I don't know why things like this have to happen. Sometimes it's a lousy world."

"Not lousy, Cody, but certainly imperfect."

"I forgot to ask you how Grandma and Grandpa are doing?"

"Grandpa still isn't feeling very well. Grandma got him to the doctor this week."

"Grandpa? I can't remember him ever going to the doctor."

Cody's mom stopped stuffing the meat loaf into the pan and gazed out the kitchen window to the backyard. "Neither can anyone else."

"What did the doctor say?"

"He ran a bunch of tests and said he'd have the results sometime next week."

"It's nothing serious, is it?" Cody asked.

"I don't think so," his mom replied. "Your granddad is seventy-five and is still trying to work like he's twenty-five. Maybe this will get him to slow down."

"Somehow I can't even imagine Grandpa slowing down."

"I can," Mrs. Clark mused. "I certainly can."

Cody felt uncomfortable and shifted his weight from boot to boot. "Did Denver take off for Missoula already?"

"Yes. He said to tell you he'd bring home a buckle for you."

"He has to beat Prescott and Reno if he wants a buckle."

"Someday he'll beat them. It just depends on who draws the best calf."

The sound of four young girls giggling and shouting in the living room almost drowned out the telephone ringing.

"Cody, my hands are covered with hamburger. Can you get that?"

He plucked up the black cordless phone. "Clark residence. What? I can't hear . . . Just a minute." He scooted down the stairs away from the noise in the living room.

The feminine voice on the phone blurted out, "Cody Wayne Clark, are you having a party at your house?"

"Feather?"

"Who were you expecting to call—Honey Del Mateo? Or is she over there now?"

"What are you talking about?"

"I'm talking about hearing several girls' voices laughing and carrying on."

"Isn't that better than hearing just one girl's voice giggling and carrying on?" Cody replied.

"Eh, yeah. You're right. What's going on?"

"It's Townie's four little sisters. They're spending the night with us," Cody explained.

"Why?"

"Have you got some time to talk?" Cody asked.

"Sure, I'm on Bruce Baxter's cell phone, and he said I could use it as much as I want."

Cody explained to Feather about Two Ponies and Sweetwater. When he finished, she didn't say anything.

"Are you still there?" he asked.

"Yeah. I was just thinking," she sighed. "I should have stayed down there."

"It's all right. Larry and I worked out some plays for the Porcupines. We'll give them our best shot."

"Oh, I know you will. And I'm doubly sorry to miss the

tournament. But what I meant was, I'm sorry I wasn't there for Townie. We're a team. We ought to be together in hard times like this."

"Larry had to go to town with his folks, so he wasn't around either. Man, talk about surprises! You'll never guess in a million years what his mom told him."

"She's pregnant?"

"What?" Cody choked. "Who told you? How did you . . ."

"Actually it was just a wild guess. Don't tell me she really is," Feather declared.

"She *is* pregnant!"

"No kidding! I can't believe it."

"Larry's pretty bummed out."

"Poor Larry."

"Did you tape the commercial yet?"

"Oh, no. We just finished a walk-through, and now I'm waiting for my costume."

"Costume? What are they going to dress you up like? A giant pizza?" Cody jibed.

"Very funny. I happen to get to wear a ballerina outfit, and I toe-dance across the houseboat and hand Bruce a large Aristocrat pizza with extra mushrooms."

"A houseboat?"

"Well, why do you think they're taping this at Coeur d'Alene Lake?"

"I didn't know you could toe-dance."

"I can't. I'm supposed to trip and fall down with my face smacking into the fresh pizza. The last scene shows me staring up at Bruce with star-shaped mushroom slices in my eyes."

"You what?"

"Oh, don't worry, they're plastic."

"What's plastic?"

"The mushroom slices."

The voice that boomed from the kitchen was not his mother's or one of the Yellowboy sisters. "Cody Wayne! I need you up here on the double."

"Hey, I've got to hang up. Dad's calling me!" Cody announced.

"Can I call you after the game?"

"Sure."

"Bye, Cody."

"Bye, Feather-girl."

With his dirty black cowboy hat pushed back, Hank Clark filled the doorway leading to the backyard. "Get your coat, hat, and spurs. A fence went down in this storm, and we've got nearly a dozen head of cattle out on the state highway."

Cody grabbed his hat and noticed all four girls lined up and staring at his dad.

"I've got a game at 6:00," he managed to blurt out.

"And I've got Denver's first year in college down there on the blacktop. He's gone, and your mom needs to watch the girls. So it's you and me, partner. Let's go get the horses."

Four

✦

An early memory Cody Clark had of his father was set in a horrible New Year's snowstorm when Cody was about three and a half. His brothers had spent that night at Grandma and Grandpa Clark's. Cody and his folks were going over there to watch the parade and football games. But the Idaho State Patrol had called in the middle of the night to say that some Clark cattle were on the highway. Travelers would not be able to keep from plowing into them during the storm.

His mother had bundled Cody up with blankets and shoved him into the cab of the pickup. She drove his dad out to the ranch, and she and Cody waited in the cab while Mr. Clark saddled and trailered a tall gray horse. Then his dad drove through the snowstorm down Badger Grade to the highway.

Cody remembered standing in the pickup seat next to his mother, who was driving along the edge of Highway 95 shining headlights on blowing snow so that his dad could round up fourteen calf-heavy cows.

Even though it was almost ten years later, Cody could still see his dad wrapped in an old yellow slicker, hunkered under a beat-up gray cowboy hat, riding that horse right into the storm. He could still feel the frigid wind blow through the sealed pickup cab and past the ineffective heater.

It took them until daylight, but he and his mom crept slowly up the grade as his dad drove the cows all the way up the mountain and into the barn. He remembered how his dad had built a big fire in the woodstove in the tack room and shoved him and his mom into the room.

His dad wouldn't come in with them though. His mom had told him years later when the subject came up that his dad's hands were too frostbitten to be put close to the fire. Later in the morning, when Cody woke up in his mother's arms, Cody's dad was at their side. His hands were wrapped in some kind of white gauze.

They hiked out of the barn to the truck and found that the storm had left two feet of fresh snow. In his mind Cody could still see a winter-bright yellow sun in the clear blue winter sky, and he could taste the lung-burning cold air.

His mother had to drive home, and they poked along, slipping and sliding in the snow. He remembered sitting cradled in his dad's arms, held by gauzed hands.

All the way to town Cody's dad had talked about the beautiful day and how gracious the Lord had been to them the night before. Not one cow was lost, and not one motorist had a wreck.

That was the day Cody realized his dad was probably the bravest man who ever lived on the face of the earth.

Nothing in the next ten years ever changed his opinion— not even when he learned that the tears in his father's eyes that day were not tears of praise but tears of extreme pain from the agony of frostbitten hands.

That was not the last storm he'd watched his dad ride off into. To Hank Clark, every animal at the ranch was a loaner from the Lord, to be taken care of well until hungry people needed to be fed.

"It's a divine privilege to be a rancher, boys," he often told them. "Any man who thinks otherwise has no reason to be in this business. A strong, healthy herd is just good stewardship—nothing more."

It was not snowing today.

It was not even still raining.

Nor was it dark.

But cows were loose near the highway. Cody's father pulled the truck into the ranch yard and backed up to the stock trailer. "You were out here this afternoon and left the barn door open?" his dad asked.

"Harriet was in the barn, and I left it open so she would come out."

"Harriet? Kind of early in the year for her to hang around a barn."

"That's what I thought."

"She still here?" Mr. Clark quizzed.

"I saw her head toward tribal land when I was about halfway back to town."

"Good. Now go saddle up Rolly and Woodrow while I hitch the trailer."

"Yes, sir."

Cody had Rolly ready and was hefting his dad's saddle to Woodrow's back when Mr. Clark entered the barn and grabbed the saddle with one hand. "Go ahead and trailer Rolly."

Within minutes they were driving down a very muddy Badger Grade road. Mr. Clark pulled off to the shoulder of the road at the stop sign. He and Cody mounted the horses. Six Black Angus cows grazed along the right-of-way on the east side of the state highway. Five cows were on the west side.

Cody's dad pointed across the highway. "I'm going to sell her."

"Which one?"

"#51."

"You think she led them down here?"

"She always does. I'm going to sell her."

"You've been saying that for five years," Cody reminded him.

Mr. Clark turned in the saddle and winked. "As soon as she starts having runty calves, I'm going to sell her."

"You want me to gather these over here?" Cody asked.

"Yeah, you ride down the edge of the highway past them, and then drive them back to the rig. Take it nice and slow. Just graze them along. I don't want them to run off."

"What then?"

"Drive 'em up the grade twenty, thirty yards and hold them. I'll bring the others over the blacktop when the traffic allows. If mine scatter, try to hold yours anyway. Don't leave them to help me unless I holler."

"What are we going to do after we get them gathered?" Cody asked.

"Drive them home. I want to put #51 in the barn overnight. Once she takes a notion to bust fences, it'll be hard to get her to change her mind."

Headlights showed cars coming half a mile up the canyon as Hank Clark walked his horse across the paved highway. "Take it slow, Cody," he called out. "And let's pray none of these yee-haws honk their horns."

Rolly was a fair roping horse, but he was a great cow horse. All Cody had to do was get the buckskin dun pointed in the right direction. The horse took over from there. Cody let the leather reins sag on Rolly's mane and just sat back and watched as the tall horse intimidated all five cows. Within fifteen minutes he had pushed them past the pickup and trailer and up the grade twenty yards. Cody bunched them in some tall grass on the cliff side of the dirt roadway.

His blanket-lined jean jacket felt warm as he turned in the saddle and watched his dad slap his coiled rope into the rump of #51. She sprinted across the paved highway, leading the other cows. He pushed them up into Cody's group.

"Good work, cowboy." His dad grinned. "You keep 'em bunched, and I'll stick Woodrow in the trailer."

"How are we going to get them to the barn?"

"You're going to drive 'em home."

"Me?"

Cody's dad pushed his hat back. "Well, you either drive

cattle or drive the truck up Badger Grade in the mud. Which will it be?"

"I'll drive the cows."

"Good choice. If #51 breaks for it, rope and dally her. If we can keep her from running off, the others will mind."

The cows seemed content to huddle in the tall brown grass as Hank Clark retreated to the trailer with Woodrow.

Cody's black beaver felt cowboy hat was pushed low on his head, and he turned the back of his collar up to block the cool breeze that blew up the canyon. The air tasted clean. The only sounds were the whine of tires on the blacktop and a restless bawl of a Black Angus cow.

Then a sudden squeal of car brakes.

A blast of a horn.

And a scream, "Hey, cowboy!"

Cow #51 sized up the moment as an opportunity to escape. She charged past Cody. He built a loop as the cow headed straight for a van full of camera-carrying tourists, who scampered out on the shoulder of the highway. While the rope circled his head, Rolly broke after the cow.

The loop sailed through the air, settled around the cow's neck, and was yanked tight by Cody's dally around the saddle horn. Rolly stopped instantly and braced himself for the jolt that would follow.

Fortunately for the cinches on Cody's saddle, the tough nylon rope, and the health of several tourists, #51 decided there was no use to test the catch. She stopped before full impact at the end of the rope, bellowed at the passing traffic, and meandered toward some tall grass next to the parked van.

The tourists applauded.

Cody's dad stepped out of the back of the stock trailer with his .30-30 carbine draped over his arm and a scowl on his face. Immediately the tourists scampered back into the van, and the driver spun gravel as they reentered the road.

Mr. Clark stormed over to Cody. "They're nuts! Would you drive up, honk your horn, and scream if a doctor was performing surgery? Or even if a barber was giving a haircut? What do they think this is—a game?"

"They thought it was a game until #51 charged them and you came out with your carbine."

Mr. Clark broke into a wide grin. "I thought I might have to shoot #51 before she ran over some tourists."

"They thought you were ready to shoot them."

"Good. Maybe they'll think twice next time."

"You think so?" Cody asked.

He shook his head. "Nope. Most folks have no idea on earth what cowboyin' is. You did a good job, son."

"I don't know what I would have done if she had tested the rope."

"Peeled tourists out of the pavement, I reckon. Take 'em home, cowboy."

"Shall I leave #51 tied?"

"As long as she behaves. If she tries something crazy, throw that rope off and keep going with the others. I'll come up behind you, and if she breaks, I'll take care of her." He looked down at the Winchester '94 carbine. "One way or another."

Five miles is a short trip in a pickup.

But it's a long way driving eight peaceful cows and one old grouch.

Cody was glad it didn't rain any more.

And that #51 had resigned herself to, at least, temporary captivity.

On a clear day the sun would have been above the tree-line to the west. However, with heavy clouds Cody was thankful for the lights of his dad's pickup as they pushed the cows into the pasture next to the big red barn.

His dad led #51 into the solid board round pen and shut the gate behind her. After tossing a couple of flakes of hay over the seven-foot fence, he helped Cody put the horses away. "Rub old Rolly down good. He did a fine job for an old boy," Cody's dad instructed. "What time did you say you had a basketball game?"

"Basketball! Oh, man . . . ," Cody choked. "I forgot all about it!"

The Clarks' GMC Suburban rolled up to the barn with headlights blinking. Two electric windows rolled down. Cody's mom was driving with the four Yellowboy girls in the backseat. "You get them put up?" she called.

"Yep. Your youngest did a good job," Cody's dad reported.

"Well, if I don't get him to a basketball game in five minutes, Larry Lewis will have a heart attack! Come on, Cody, I've got your gear in the back. You can change on the way to town."

Cody dove into the rig. His mother spun gravel as she raced back down toward County Line Road.

"Where am I supposed to change?" Cody called out.

"Behind the backseat," his mother replied.

Cody climbed over the seat and then looked up to see four wide-eyed girls staring at him.

"Mom, tell them not to look!"

"Come on, girls, everyone pile into the front seat with me."

"He's rather shy, isn't he?" Alena offered.

"I think of it as tastefully timid," his mother replied.

Cody leaped out of the Suburban as it rolled to a stop next to the concrete steps of the Halt High School gym and sprinted into the building. Neither shoe was tied. He could feel the tag of his tie-dyed, sleeveless T-shirt rub the front of his neck.

This is the worst prepared I've ever been for a game in my life.

Larry Lewis paced the sidelines and almost cried when he saw Cody trot in. "Man, that's cutting it too close, Clark! Two more minutes, and Dad said I had to forfeit."

"I had to round up some cattle."

"Well, tie your shoes and turn your shirt around. Quick! We've got a game to play."

"I take it the Pine Creek Porcupines know we aren't exactly at full strength."

"They do now. But at least I won the toss."

"Hey, Cody," Tim Sharpe called out, "where's the rest of your team?"

"We gave them the night off. I told them to rest up for the championship game," Larry spouted.

"Very funny. You guys can't play us with two."

Larry bounced the ball out to Cody, who quickly shot

it back. Dribbling the ball, Larry spun back toward the basket, drawing the expected double-team. But instead of continuing the drive, he raced away from the basket. Both defenders waited for the other one to pursue, leaving Larry alone with the ball for a split second.

Bad choice.

Nothing but net.

On the first possession, Jim Thunder was the open man and broke to the hoop. Larry faked pursuit, leaving Tim Sharpe. The ball was lobbed over to Tim, but Larry dove in front of it and knocked it over to Cody, who dribbled behind the line and then drove for the right side. The three confused Pine Creek Porcupines converged on him.

It was a simple bounce-pass over to Larry.

Another bucket.

The Porcupines called a time-out.

Larry and Cody converged near center court.

Cody leaned over and rested his hand on his knees. "I don't think they'll make those mistakes again."

"Hey, my plans did work!"

"And if they fake their passes and keep spread out, we'll never stop their offense," Cody warned.

"I'll match them shot for shot now. We've got them by four."

The abbreviated version of the Lewis and Clark Squad did match them shot for shot. The only problem was that the Porcupines' shots were mostly unmissable lay-ins. The Squad was shooting heavily guarded jumpers.

When the score reached 14 to 6 with the Squad losing, Larry called a time-out.

"I think we need something new, cowboy."

"I need some new legs. First, that bike ride home and then gathering the cattle. I'm worn out."

"I'm going to run #1 again, only I'll fake the basketball back out to you and then drive on to the basket."

"You know they'll have you double-teamed."

"Two-on-one? That sounds about even to me. Maybe we'll catch them flat-footed."

"Maybe you'll catch an elbow across the nose," Cody cautioned. "Anyway, how are we going to stop their offense?"

"Let's press them," Larry suggested.

"What?"

"They won't be expecting us to guard them close. Sharpe always brings the ball in. Let's charge right at him and the Thunder kid—real in-your-face-basketball. Maybe they'll panic and make a bad toss. We don't have a lot of options here, Clark."

"I believe that's the first time I've ever heard you say that."

Larry's faked pass back out to Cody was classic. The Porcupine double-team stood stunned as Larry wove between them and finger-rolled the ball into the net.

The quick press resulted in a quick turnover. This time Larry was triple-teamed. Sharpe snuck up from the blind side and knocked the ball away. But it bounced to where Cody stood, behind the three-point line. With two Pine Creek Porcupines sprinting toward him, he tossed up a hurried shot that slammed into the glass and then sailed through the net.

"All right, 14 to 11!" Larry hollered. "Now the teams are at even strength."

"How do you figure that?" Tim Sharpe growled.

"We've got Big Mo on our team."

"Momentum? Not for long!" Sharpe insisted.

The Porcupines kept a wide triangle and passed the ball around like a lopsided game of keep-away. When Cody broke for the dribbler, Thunder sprinted to the basket. It was a wide open lay-in, and all Cody could do now was trail along two steps behind.

But for the first time all night, the Porcupines blew an easy shot. Cody grabbed the rebound and fired it overhand to Larry, who drained a jump shot over Sharpe's outstretched hands.

About half of the spectators cheered. The other half were engrossed in the girls' league game running at the same time at the other end of the court.

This time the Porcupines did not miss the shot.

But the Lewis and Clark Squad did.

Twice.

The score was 18 to 14 when Larry called for their last time-out.

"They'll give us a two just to get the ball back," Larry cautioned. "We need a couple threes."

"I've made my one lucky shot of the night. Don't count on me for another three."

"We need Townie or Feather," Larry insisted.

"That would be nice."

"Here's what we're going to do," Larry explained. "You stand still at the top of the key and do nothing."

"I can handle that."

"I'll just run back and forth along the three-point line. They'll figure you'll try to screen them, but don't even fake it. Just stand there. I'll try to get as many of them chasing me as I can. Then on my tenth lap you set the pick, and I'll take a quick three-pointer."

"How about the seventh lap?" Cody suggested.

"Why seven?"

"'Cause that's how many times the Hebrews went around Jericho before it fell."

"All right, we're bringing down some walls! I like that."

Cody positioned himself at the top of the key with his back to the basket and watched as Larry Lewis put on a dribbling demonstration. Back and forth he went, using every step and dribble he had ever learned. At first the Porcupines were content just to let him dribble back and forth. But after the crowd started to mumble, one Porcupine and then another followed him in pursuit.

Cody counted laps. *Five . . . six . . . this is it!*

Several steps before Larry reached him, Cody turned and set his arms across his chest. Larry cut close, and Sharpe and Thunder plowed into Cody. All three boys tumbled to the polished wood floor.

Brian Tasker left the key and leaped to try to block Larry's shot. But a quick pump fake, and Tasker stumbled to the floor.

Larry alone was standing as he sailed up with a spinning Spalding. The net popped and bounced when the ball dropped through.

"We did it, Cody Wayne! Now let's stop them on defense!" Larry cried out.

Cody pulled himself to his feet. "What's the call, coach?"

Larry shoved Cody toward the key. "You play zone. Don't let anyone take an uncontested shot in the paint."

"And you?"

"I'll guard Tim one-on-one. He's the only three-point threat they have."

The Porcupines brought the ball in cautiously. Sharpe and Thunder stayed above the three-point line, while Brian Tasker huddled under the basket next to Cody.

Four times Jim Thunder stood unguarded above the line with ball in hand, but every time he passed it off. The fifth time Tim Sharpe screamed, "Drive it!"

Jim Thunder dribbled straight to the right side.

"Stay in the paint, Cody Wayne!" Larry screamed.

Cody hung back, and Brian Tasker scrambled around to block him out.

"Now!" Larry yelled.

Cody spun around Tasker and leaped at the same time. His right hand slapped into the hard synthetic leather basketball, bouncing it high into the stands.

"Yes!" Larry yelled.

"It's still their ball, L. B.," Cody cautioned.

Larry trotted by and mumbled, "Let's press them again."

"And leave Brian under the hoop?"

"Come on!" Larry called out.

Cody's tired legs lumbered after Jim Thunder, his basketball shoes slapping the slick wood floor. With his arms stretched high, Cody leaped one more time. Thunder, seeing a clear shot to Tasker filled with a flailing Cody Clark, panicked and sent a hurried pass right back to Tim Sharpe.

That move was exactly what Larry had anticipated. He jumped in front of Sharpe and stole the ball.

"You two drop back and play zone. I'll take Lewis!" Tim Sharpe called out. Larry dribbled back and forth above the three-point line. Sharpe hung close enough to keep him from a clear shot but back far enough that Larry couldn't drive around him.

Cody had to come out to the free-throw line to have any chance at a pass. Whenever he did get one, the other two Porcupines converged on him quickly. All he could do was dribble back out to the three-point line and dump the ball off to Larry.

After three cycles of the same routine, Cody took the pass at the top of the key and hollered to Larry, "Take your best shot, partner. You can do it!" *Man, I hope this works!*

This time Cody faked the pass to Larry. Thunder and Tasker leaned forward to block the pass, but at the last minute Cody yanked the ball back. Lurching forward, he split the defenders and drove to the hoop. All three Porcupines panicked and rumbled after him. With a no-look pass, Cody flipped the ball straight back over the top of his head.

Larry caught the ball and dribbled one step back behind the three-point line. Over the outstretched arms and the top-of-the-lungs "NO!" of Tim Sharpe, Larry shot.

His right wrist flipped the ball forward with perfect form, and his fingers trailed straight toward the basket.

Sharpe clapped his hands together and shouted again, "No!"

Larry threw his hands in the air.

Cody held his breath from under the basket.

The ball circled the orange rim once, dipped into the net, and then popped out of the basket as if some unseen magnetic force rejected its presence.

The crowd moaned.

Larry stood stunned.

The Porcupines cheered.

Cody dove for the loose ball.

It bounced off his hand, crashed into Tasker's knee, and rolled out of bounds.

"Our ball, L. B.!" Cody shouted.

Larry continued to stand with his right hand above his head in perfect follow-through. "I can't believe I missed that shot!" he mumbled. "I just can't believe it!"

The ball rolled under the bleachers. Cody struggled several minutes to retrieve it. He brought it to the baseline.

Larry continued to wander around the three-point line mumbling to himself.

"Larry, snap out of it! We've got to get the ball in play," Cody yelled.

"I can't believe it!" Larry muttered as Sharpe and Thunder closely guarded him. "How could I miss that shot?"

Then out of the corner of his eye, Cody saw the most wonderful vision—like an angel suddenly appearing to offer deliverance. Only this angel wore an orange and yellow tie-dyed T-shirt and a wide grin across his dark brown face. Larry ran forward to take the pass and was triple-teamed when Cody sailed the ball over all of their heads to the gum-chewing figure at the top of the key.

"No!" Larry yelled.

Jeremiah Yellowboy took the pass and stared at the back rim of the basket. Without raising a foot off the ground, he tossed a high arcing shot toward the hoop.

Nothing but net.

And confusion.

"We won! We won!" Larry shouted.

"That's illegal!" the Pine Street Porcupines screamed.

Cody ran to Jeremiah and threw an arm around his shoulder. "I thought you were in Denver!"

"That doesn't count!" Tim Sharpe yelled. "They had an illegal player on the court!"

Everyone in the stands was buzzing.

"I didn't make it to Denver. They only had one standby, and my mom took it. She sent me back home. I called Grandpa before I left Salt Lake, and he met me in Lewiston and drove me home."

"Man, you showed up in time!" Cody hollered.

"It's our ball!" Jim Thunder yelled. "Get off the court, Yellowboy. You're not in this game! It's our ball. The game isn't over. It's not over!"

Thunder took the basketball and threw it in to Tim Sharpe, who stood alone under the basket. He tossed in the uncontested lay-in.

"We won!" Sharpe screamed. "Your basket didn't count! It didn't count!"

The shrill whistle came from Mr. Lewis, who trotted over with Mr. Ketchum, the principal.

"They cheated!" Sharpe called out. "It doesn't count. We won, right?"

Mr. Lewis turned to the principal. "I'll let Mr. Ketchum call this one since Larry's on the team."

Mr. Ketchum, with trademark short-sleeved white shirt and butch haircut, loosened his navy blue tie and unbuttoned the top button on his shirt.

"All right, boys, listen up."

Both teams huddled around the two men who stood on the free-throw line.

"Let's review some rules for summer three-on-three league. It's legal to play with two players, right, Coach Lewis?"

"Minimum of two, maximum of three on the court at any one time."

"But you don't have to use three even if you have them in attendance," the principal continued.

"Correct."

"And Mr. Yellowboy is on the roster as a member of the Squad?"

Coach Lewis pointed to his clipboard. "Oh, yes. He hasn't missed a game."

"And players can only enter a game during a time-out, after a made shot, or when play is stopped."

"Like digging a ball out from under the bleachers," Larry added.

"That's correct," his father affirmed.

"So Mr. Yellowboy's entry into the game was perfectly legal," Mr. Ketchum concluded.

"But no one came out! If you send a player in, someone has to come out!" Sharpe fumed.

"Not if the team is less than full strength," Coach Lewis countered. "Tim, last week Brian was two minutes late for your game, and you started without him."

"Our car broke down coming home from Lewiston," Brian Tasker explained.

Coach Lewis continued, "And you brought him into the game when Donnie Barnes tossed that air ball up on the stage."

"But that was different. That was at the first of the game!"

"It's the same rule," Mr. Ketchum explained. "Jeremiah was perfectly legal to enter the game when he did. The victory goes to the Lewis and Clark Squad."

"All right!" Larry hollered.

"I can't believe this," Tim Sharpe groaned. "You didn't beat us; you conned us out of that last shot!"

"Think of it this way," Brian Tasker conceded. "At least we don't have to play J. J. and Ty!"

Five

◉

Cody dragged himself out of his bed, staggered over a snoring Jeremiah Yellowboy perched on top of a sleeping bag on the floor, and then wobbled down the hallway toward the kitchen. A battered pair of nylon Nike shorts and a sleeveless black California Rodeo T-shirt had served as his pajamas. The fluorescent light seemed unbearably bright.

He squinted at his mother. "Did you say I have a telephone call?"

"It's Larry. He said it's an emergency."

"What kind of emergency?"

"You ask him."

"But we were going to sleep in late."

"It is late," she declared.

"What time is it?"

"7:15."

"That's not late! Townie and me played Risk until . . . eh, it was—"

"It was 12:18, I believe, when you turned your light out," she informed him.

"Oh, yeah, I knew it was something like that."

"Talk to Larry."

"He's still on the line?"

"Unless he fell asleep or decided to write a novel while he's waiting."

Cody slumped on a stool at the counter and banged the hard plastic black cordless phone to his ear.

"Yeah?" he mumbled.

"Cody?"

"What's the emergency, Lewis?"

"It's awful!"

"What's awful?"

"Have you heard what happened?"

"Have I heard? Until two minutes ago I was dreaming about gathering Texas longhorn cattle."

"A nightmare, huh?"

"No, it wasn't a nightmare. But I'm going to hang up if you don't tell me whatever it was you called me about."

"What's the worst thing on earth that could happen?" Larry's high-pitched voice quizzed.

"In *your* mind?"

"Yeah."

"Someone discovered that Larry Bird graduated from Kentucky, not Indiana State."

"Get real. Guess again."

"The University of Indiana decided to drop men's basketball."

"You're delirious, Clark. Meaningless words are dribbling out of your mouth. Guess again. What's the worst thing imaginable here in Halt?"

"Having someone call me at 7:15 in the morning when I wanted to sleep late."

"Come on . . . guess."

"Larry, I'm hanging up."

"The gym's ruined!"

Cody pulled the phone away from his ear, stared at it for a minute, and then replaced it. "What did you say?"

"You know that big rainstorm we had in the middle of the night—thunder, lightning, and all that?"

"We had a storm last night?"

"About two o'clock. Did you hear it?"

"I guess not."

"Well, water seeped through the gym ceiling and puddled up on the basketball floor."

"Really?"

"Yeah, my dad and mom are over there now trying to help the janitors mop up the water."

"What does this mean?" Cody quizzed.

"The championship game is postponed."

"We don't have a game today?"

"Nope."

"When will we?"

"Dad says we'll have to wait and see what damage there might be after the floors dry. He's going to put some fans and heaters in there so it might be all right by tomorrow night—if they can keep the roof from leaking again. Is that bum news, or what?"

"Oh, I don't know. I'm so tired from yesterday I could use the rest. Besides, Feather might be back by tomorrow night. It would be good to have full strength."

"Yeah," Larry pondered, "you might be right. And it gives us another day to practice!"

"No! It gives us a day to sleep in!" Cody countered.

"I suppose this means you and Townie don't want to come over now and run some plays."

"At 7:15 A.M.?"

"It's 7:21."

"Go to sleep, Larry."

"I can't sleep. I laid in my bed all night staring at the ceiling. I can't believe I missed that open shot, Cody. It's like my whole career went out the window with that missed shot. If I can't make the easy ones . . . I don't know. I just can't believe it."

"Maybe the Lord is trying to tell you something," Cody proposed.

"Like what?"

"Like maybe you still have some things to learn, and He . . . you know, is still in charge of things, not you."

Larry paused for a while before answering. "You really think so?"

"I know He's telling me I ought to get some more sleep. I'll talk to you later, L. B."

Cody shut off the phone and shuffled toward the brown-carpeted hallway.

"Did I hear you say your basketball game is canceled?"

"The roof at the gym leaked. They have to dry it out before we can play. Larry said it would be tomorrow night at the earliest."

"Well, that's interesting. Dad and I were saying this

morning that if you didn't have that big game, we'd like to drive up to Spokane and watch the boys rodeo."

"Today? What about Townie and the girls?"

"Their granddad is picking up the girls at 9:00 A.M. to meet their Aunt Lucy in Colfax. Jeremiah's staying with us until Carmen tells us something different. He can go with us."

"When would we leave?"

"If we can get away, we'll leave before 10:00 A.M. The boys' first go is during the slack at 1:30 P.M., and the second go is at 7:30."

"Would we spend the night?" Cody asked.

"We'll drive back late."

"Will Prescott and Reno be able to come home with us?"

"No, they have to go to Ellensburg for a two o'clock show tomorrow."

"Can Larry come with us?"

"Only if he promises not to dribble his basketball inside the Suburban," Margaret Clark replied. "You know how that gives your father a headache."

"This is great! We haven't seen them rope since Jordan Valley!" Cody trudged toward the stairs. "But I think I'll sleep another hour."

"I think you'd better get dressed and ride out and feed Eureka's horses."

"But, Mom, I'm really, really tired!"

"I bet you are, Cody Wayne. It's a good lesson to learn."

"What lesson is that?"

"Whatever you sow, that you shall reap."

"Can I sleep on the drive to Spokane?"

"If you can sleep with Larry and Jeremiah in the rig, more power to you. Now go on. Get dressed and feed those horses. The cool air will wake you up."

It was exactly three miles from Cody's backyard to Eureka's horse barn. County Line Road was mostly gravel and packed mud, especially after a rain. It followed the up-and-down contour of the high mountain prairie and forest.

Clouds still covered the north-central Idaho sky, but they were higher and much less threatening than the day before. In scattered places Cody could see a backdrop of bright blue.

Water puddled along the side of the road, but the crown was no longer sticky, and Cody was glad not to be flinging up a trail of mud. He was happy to have his coat buttoned and white cotton roping gloves on his hands. His braided horsehair stampede string was yanked tight under his chin, keeping his black cowboy hat screwed down on his head.

His thigh and calf muscles ached every time he had to climb a hill, and he shifted into the easiest gear. Sunlight broke through the cracks in the clouds, and when he turned onto the dirt road to the west, he could see a bright beam reflecting off the Clark barn.

It's been a great summer, Lord. I never knew I'd spend so much time out at the ranch playing basketball. When I

*grow up and somebody asks what it was like growing up
in Idaho, this will probably be the summer I tell them about.*

Townie.

Larry.

Feather.

And me.

You took four loners and made a team.

The Squad.

*But once school starts, it will be different. Short days.
Bus rides. Homework. Seeing J. J. every day in the hallway
and at the lockers.*

*Feather and Larry will have to meet everyone at school.
I wonder which girls Feather will be friends with? Maybe
Julie G. and Julie B. Except they giggle a lot.*

Feather doesn't giggle.

As much.

He leaned his bike against Eureka Blaine's faded gray
barn door and strolled over to the empty practice roping
arena. He climbed up on the bottom rail and peered at the
dirt and mud. Then he held up his clenched fist like a
microphone and shouted: "Our next calf-roper, folks, will
be Prescott Clark from Halt, Idaho. He'll be followed by
Reno Clark, then by Denver Clark, and finally by Cody
Clark! These boys come from a great rodeo family. Some
of you older folks might remember a talented Idaho roper
by the name of Hank Clark back in the late sixties. Well,
he married a mighty purdy barrel racer by the name of
Margaret Sweet, and these are their boys. It's a good thing
they pay six places at this rodeo, or the rest of the boys

could just go on down the road. Let's hear a warm welcome to Idaho's first family of rodeo—the Clarks!"

Hurray! Hurray! And the crowd goes wild!

Lord, it's a nice dream.

Even if it won't ever happen.

Cody hiked over to the horse barn and scooped up an empty white plastic bucket. An object next to the open door caused him to stop and drop the bucket.

"That looks like . . ." He reached down to pick up the 6-x-8-inch scrap of simulated leather. "It is! It's a piece of Larry's basketball!"

Cody peeked into the dark shadows of the barn. Spying a pick handle, he grabbed it and slung it over his shoulder like a baseball bat.

"Harriet, I know you're in Eureka's barn. You come out of there right now!"

From deep in the darkness he heard a rattle of teeth.

"Yeah, I'm talking to you. I'm in a hurry and don't have time to play tag like we did yesterday. Now get out of there!" he hollered.

There was a snort.

"Harriet!"

From out of the shadows the javelina began to charge him. He lifted the stout hickory handle above his head.

"I'll bust you in the snout if you come after me! You know I'll do it."

The peccary stopped with a yap and a squeal.

"Now go on—get out of here!" Cody insisted.

The gray furball in a pig's suit lifted her nose a couple of times and held her ground.

Without lowering the raised pick handle or taking his eyes off Harriet, Cody squatted down and snatched up the worn brown synthetic leather fragment formerly known as Larry Lewis's basketball. He tossed it at the javelina.

"Here, take your treasure and go!"

Harriet rattled her teeth, snorted, scooped up the ragged-edged portion that still read "Spa-," and trotted out into the yard between the barn and Eureka's single-wide mobile home.

Cody watched her short little legs scoot down the winding driveway toward the dirt road that separated the Clark ranch from the Blaine ranch. When she scampered across the road toward the red barn, Cody screamed, "Don't you go in our barn!"

The javelina stopped and stared back at him.

"You heard me!" he hollered. "Stay out of the barns!"

Harriet turned west and trotted toward the thick forest of pines and tamaracks.

"Thank you!"

He reentered the barn and scooped up some rolled oats. *That's the only time in my life that she ever minded me. I wonder if she's sick or something? It doesn't seem right for her to want to hang around the barns already. Maybe it's going to be a really early winter.*

Larry and Jeremiah were waiting on the back step of the Clark house when Cody came pumping his bike up the dirt alley.

"It's rodeo time!" Jeremiah hurrahed.

"Did your grandpa take the girls already?" Cody asked.

"Yep. And my mom called."

"What's happening? How are your brothers doing?"

"Mom said Two Ponies is burned the worst—all over his arms, face, and chest. His hair is all gone."

"How about Sweetwater?"

"It ends up he's burned mostly on his legs. She was pretty happy. They upgraded him to critical."

"That's good?" Larry croaked.

"That's better than Two Ponies. But she said the doctors are encouraged about him, too. She said they were both in such good physical shape that the shock of the fire didn't seem to affect anything on the inside. It hit them and passed on so quick that they didn't get enough smoke in their lungs to kill them."

"What happens if they—," Larry stammered, "I mean, I'm sure they're going to pull out of it fine, but what kind of recovery will they need?"

"They could be there up to six months," Jeremiah explained.

"Whoa . . . what does that mean for your mom?" Cody quizzed.

"She was talking about staying in Denver with them."

"What about you and the girls?" Cody probed.

"The girls can stay with Aunt Lucy, and I . . ."

"You could stay with us," Cody offered.

"Mom said she'd like me to come be with her in Denver."

"And miss school?" Larry challenged.

"I guess I'd go to school there."

Cody jammed his hands into his jeans jacket pockets. "That would be different."

"That would be scary. Anyway, she said we wouldn't make that kind of decision for a week or so—after the doctors get a better idea of the schedule for skin grafts for my brothers."

"Man, that's tough," Cody added.

"I'll worry about it later. Today I'm feeling pretty good. Yesterday at this time I thought my brothers were dead or dying. Now it looks like they'll pull through. It would be ungrateful to God not to feel good today. Right, Cody?"

"Yeah. That's probably true every day, isn't it?"

"Personally, I'm disappointed," Larry inserted. "I really wanted to play that championship game today."

Cody's dad, smelling of aftershave and wearing his Black Gold Resistol cowboy hat, stepped outside. "Time to load up, boys!"

"I get to sit by the window!" Cody called.

"Me, too!" Jeremiah echoed.

"Hey, I'll take the middle," Larry offered. "It's probably best. I've worked up some new plays that ought to catch the Pirates by surprise. If I'm in the middle, both of you can see the charts."

Jeremiah rolled his eyes.

"Hey, Dad," Cody called out, "can we strap Larry to the luggage rack?"

The Spokane Interstate Fairgrounds rodeo arena was mostly empty when the Clark Suburban pulled into the dirt parking lot. Hank and Margaret Clark headed to the rodeo secretary's office to visit with some longtime friends. Cody led Jeremiah and Larry to the concession stand and then into the covered but fairly empty bleachers.

"I don't get this 'slack' thing." Larry flopped down on the wooden seat with a chili dog in his right hand. "You compete without anyone watching, and it counts just like the regular performance?"

Cody bit into a hot and spicy German sausage dog and then wiped the corner of his mouth with the back of his hand. "Yeath," he mumbled, then swallowed hard. "They don't have time in the regular performance to run everyone who wants to compete. So some of them make their run now. They have the same judges and timers but not much audience."

"But it's kind of dull competing with no one in the stands, isn't it?"

"In this rodeo they have two runs to make. They work off a combined score. One of the runs will be with the stands full. So it's about the same for everyone."

"Are your brothers here yet? I've never met Reno and Prescott," Larry inquired.

"I don't think they will be here until just about 1:00. They were driving up from a rodeo in Missoula."

"Do they know we're coming?" Jeremiah questioned.

"Nope. They think everyone's at home going to our championship basketball game."

Larry carefully negotiated a hotdog rounded with onions, pickles, tomatoes, and yellow cheese slivers into his mouth. When he chomped down, mustard squirted out the corners of his lips. A swipe of a white paper napkin removed 90 percent of the mustard. "This is almost but not quite as good as a Hoosier Dog."

"A Hoosier Dog?" Jeremiah groaned. "Is everything better in Indiana?"

"Oh, no." Larry grinned. "Actually the skiing is pretty lousy, and the surfing isn't worth squat."

Jeremiah used his fingernail to pick a piece of hotdog bun from between his teeth. "Listen, L. B., if it's so great in Indiana, why did you move to Idaho?"

"Just to make sure everyone here understands what they are missing."

"And we're grateful for that," Cody laughed.

"Thank you. Thank you very much." Larry turned his hotdog around and bit it from the other end. "Dmptht yrrm aber."

"He speaking in Hoosierese?" Jeremiah hooted.

"No, I think it's hotdogolian."

"What I was trying to say," Larry gulped, "was did you guys ever wonder what J. J. and those guys do on a free day?"

"Nope. I never thought about it," Cody admitted.

"I always assumed they went out and kicked little dogs or practiced chewing nails or something like that," Jeremiah laughed.

"Well, I've been worrying. What if they spend the whole day working up a brand-new offense to use against us?" Larry stewed.

"Why would they? The old one has beat us twice, and Ty is taller than Rocky."

"Yeah, you're probably right. You know what? I hope next summer we're so good other teams have to sit around worried about how to beat us."

"Next summer? That would be cool to have the same team," Cody remarked.

"We'd dominate them," Larry insisted.

"Even if I have to go to Denver for a few months, I'd be back by then . . . I think." Jeremiah hesitated. "Hey, isn't that your dad out in the arena?"

Cody glanced up to see his tall, broad-shouldered, graying father strolling across the freshly worked, slightly wet dirt of the arena. "Hey, Cody, Mom got talked into being the assistant timer, and I'm going to help the chute boss. Will you three be all right?"

"Yes, sir!" Cody shouted back.

"Well, don't go running off with any buckle bunnies!" He grinned and headed for the south end of the arena.

Cody slumped down in the bleachers. *I can't believe he said that!*

"What are buckle bunnies?" Larry asked.

"Never mind," Cody mumbled. "Hey, there's Eureka!"

"The guy whose horses you feed?"

"I forgot he'd be up here," Cody declared. "He has his calvin' horses and doggin' horses here."

"Doggin' horses?" Larry shook his head. "I'm a stranger in a foreign land."

"See that yella horse?" Cody pointed to the far end of the arena.

"Yellow? None of the horses are yellow," Larry objected.

"He meant the dark cream-colored one," Jeremiah explained.

"Yeah . . . what about it?"

"It's one of Eureka's best. It's called Britches, but its real name is Slash Bar Jake."

"Its real name?" Larry shook his head. "I'm going to get a Mountain Dew. . . . You want me to bring you something?"

"I'd like a plate of coconut macaroon cookies," Jeremiah joked.

"Yeah, right!" Larry wandered down the wooden stairs toward the concession stand.

Jeremiah beat his bag of potato chips flat and then poured the crumbs over his second hotdog. His teeth crunched into it. After several chomps and a swallow, he looked over at Cody. "What time will it take to win?"

"The first go?"

"Yeah."

"At least 9.5. They'll have to break 10 to be in the money."

"Ought to be some good ropin'."

"With three Clark brothers? Man, you know there'll be some good ropin'."

Jeremiah sat up and pointed across the empty stands to the far end of the arena. "Isn't that Reno?"

"Hey, they made it! And that's Prescott on Britches." Cody noticed Jeremiah grab a napkin and wipe the corner of his eyes.

"You all right, Townie?"

"Yeah . . . just some arena dust."

"You thinking about Two Ponies and Sweetwater?"

Jeremiah let out a deep breath. "It's kind of nice having older brothers, isn't it?"

"It sure is!" Cody left his food lying on the worn wooden bleacher and scampered down to the railing.

"Reno!" he hollered and waved.

The cowboy in the dusty black hat and blue and white long-sleeved cowboy shirt rode toward him.

"Cody Wayne . . . I hear you made the championship game but had it postponed!"

"How did you guys do in Missoula last night?" Cody asked.

"We're sitting first in Team Roping, and Prescott's in the money with calves. We'll see how those times hold. Denver had a calf jerk loose and kick him above the eye."

"Is he okay?"

"Oh, yeah. Some purdy little blonde nurse fussed over him most of the evenin'." Reno turned his horse back to the south end of the arena and then leaned back with his hand on the horse's rump. "Where's that lil' darlin' of yours I've been hearin' about all summer?"

"My what?" Cody choked.

"You mean Feather?" Jeremiah grinned. "She's an actress and is on location filming a scene with Bruce Baxter."

"No foolin'? Lil' bro' has himself an actress?"

"She's not really my girlfriend, Reno. We're just good friends."

"Listen, I'm your brother, not your mother. You can level with me."

"I am leveling with you," Cody fussed.

Jeremiah coughed. "Actually Cody and Feather have a thing going."

"I knew it!" Reno hooted.

"I don't even know what a 'thing' is!" Cody wailed.

"Well, I've got to go to work, boys. If we don't pick up speed between now and Pendleton, we'll be coming home early this year."

With so few people in the stands, Cody, Larry, and Jeremiah hung out by the rail and watched the calf-roping.

Prescott's calf ran on him, and he had to settle with a 10.8. Reno's calf was a kicker, and he lost a little time on the wrap. Denver had a perfect run of 9.2, but he broke the barrier and ended up with a 19.2.

They all met later in the back room of Earl's Texas Ribs and Prairie Chicken Cafe, six blocks from the fairgrounds. It was the first time the whole Clark clan had been together since Mother's Day. The air was filled with rodeo stories, past and present, and plenty of laughter.

During one fairly quiet moment when most were devouring cheesecake, Larry said, "Mrs. Clark, you're the only girl here!"

Cody saw his mother's eyes sparkle, the tan creases in the corners melting away. "Yes, here I am surrounded by seven handsome men. Most girls would die for a chance like this. I love it, Larry. It makes me feel like a queen. Of course," she said, clearing her throat, "someday I would like to have some daughters-in-law."

"Whoa! That's your cue, Prescott," Reno teased.

"Me?"

"Yeah," Denver added, "you're the oldest. You need to set a good example."

"If you guys are waitin' for me, it will be a long haul. I'm puttin' my money on lil' brother. I hear he's learnin' a lot this summer."

"No, I'm not!" Cody tried to holler above the laughter of his brothers, but he finally gave up and plunged into the cheesecake.

The arena was crammed with rodeo fans by 7:00. Cody's folks weren't needed to help during the regular performance, so they sat behind Cody, Larry, and Jeremiah, near the roping end of the arena, straight across from the bucking chutes.

The crowd was surprised when the mystery guest singer of the national anthem turned out to be Bruce Baxter.

"I didn't know he could sing," Mrs. Clark whispered.

When the a cappella anthem was over, Cody's dad replied, "He can't!"

Cody spent most of the early part of the rodeo explaining each event to Larry. When it came to the calf-roping, Cody's mom carefully recorded each time in her rodeo program. Denver burst out of the box and tied his calf in 10 seconds even.

"How come your brothers don't ride one after another?" Larry asked.

"They all want to ride Britches, but you can't ride a horse back to back. So they spread them out."

"It looks like Gilbert Alizeo drew out," Mrs. Clark announced as she studied her program. "Reno said he hurt his right shoulder, and I don't see him down here anywhere. His mother and I traveled together for two seasons."

Prescott's calf raced a bit, but he flew down the rope and tossed and tied him for a 9.4.

"Your brother's fast!" Larry exclaimed.

"That's why the Cubs drafted him to play center field."

"What? Your brother was drafted for the Cubs?"

"Yeah, but he turned them down."

"What round was he drafted in?" Larry quizzed.

"Sixth."

"You're kidding me, right?"

"No, why?"

"Who would turn down a professional baseball career for rodeo?"

"I would," Cody insisted.

Larry whistled and rolled his eyes toward the pavilion ceiling. "It must be a disease."

The announcer filled in while the chute boss scurried to fix a broken barrier string.

"Next up will be the third of the Clark brothers, Reno Clark. After him will be Texas cowboy, L. D. Saloan. That will conclude the calf-ropin' competition tonight. One cowboy had to drop out due to an injury. Now, folks, that means we have an extra calf in the chute tonight, and we've got a little exhibition scheduled for you. You get to be the ones to see it for the first time."

Cody leaned over to Jeremiah. "I bet good ol' Bruce Baxter is going to try to rope a calf."

"You think so?"

"Who else can it be?" Cody pondered.

The speakers crackled as the announcer continued, "That's right, for the first time in history four Clark brothers are going to compete. The youngest of the clan, thirteen-year-old Cody Clark, is here with us tonight, and he has agreed to rope that last calf for us in an exhibition run!"

Six

●

*T*wice before Cody had experienced a similar feeling. The first time was that New Year's Day in the white-out blizzard, watching his father gather cattle off the highway. The whole event was displayed like a big-screen television with wrap-around sound. He was a part of the spectacle and yet an observer, too.

The second time was in the first grade when Honey Del Mateo put her soft lips on his and kissed him next to the bleachers in the Halt High School gym. It was like he could see the entire scene, not from his limited viewpoint but from a camera mounted high in the rafters. He could see her face and his face, her smile and his smile, all at the same time.

And now in a rodeo arena in Spokane, Washington, he could see himself blush in the stands. See his mother, father, Larry, and Townie push him toward the aisle. He could see the young cowboy with black hat and scruffy brown Justin Ropers climb the arena fence and trot across the dirt and mud until he reached his brothers who loomed above him.

He could see Denver hand him a rope and two pigging strings, Prescott unstrap his spurs and shove them his direction, and Eureka Blaine slap him on the back.

He was there sitting on the top rail between Denver and Prescott as they watched Reno rope, but it was almost like being in a blimp high above the arena. Reno's time was 8.9 and would put him in first place, with only one more roper to go.

When Mr. L. D. Saloan from Stephenville, Texas, backed into the box, Cody felt his own left foot slip into the stirrup, and reality hit him like a summer squall.

"Denver, adjust those stirrups!" Prescott called out.

"Britches knows when you're supposed to throw. He'll get ticked if you wait too long!" Eureka counseled.

"Your steer ran left in the slack," Reno called out. "Loop him before he cuts."

"That barrier string is tight as a fiddle—you can bust it with the wind," Denver added. "Prescott, tighten that cinch. Britches was just holdin' his breath."

"Flank him on the run and use your momentum," Prescott counseled. "If you have to chase him around the end of a rope, you'll never get him to the dirt. These aren't junior calves."

"Don't nod until Britches's ears are both pointed at the far end of the arena. Be patient," Eureka added.

"Well, let's give the Texas cowboy a Washington round of applause because that's all he's going to take home tonight. There was no score on that run," the announcer blared.

"You won, Reno!" Cody called out from the saddle.

"What? Oh, yeah, good. Now listen, little bro', no shortcuts. I want to see two full wraps before the hooey."

"Right."

Denver reached up and slapped him on the leg. "Make us proud."

"Shoot," Prescott said grinning, "I'm mighty proud already."

"Stick him, cowboy!" Reno hooted.

Cody stood in the stirrups and rode Britches out in front of the roping box. He tucked one coiled pigging string into his belt, and the other he adjusted in his mouth. Then he built a loop and tucked the rope under his right arm. Finally, he rode Britches into the box on the east side of the calf chute and turned him around. While the chute boss attached the barrier string, Cody tugged on the reins twice, and Britches backed into the far corner.

Cody reached up and yanked down the front brim of his black felt cowboy hat. He glanced over at the man at the chute who was waiting for his signal.

"Watch his ears!" Eureka Blaine hollered.

Cody spied the cream-colored horse's left ear pointed toward the far end of the arena, but the right ear was tilted back toward Cody.

"Get that ear pointed around right now!" Cody barked. "Don't you try to listen to me! You go when you feel my spurs, understand?"

Britches shuffled his feet, snorted, and raised his

nose. Cody leaned forward and slapped the horse's head twice. "Get it down!"

Britches dropped his head, and both ears flipped toward the far end of the arena.

Lord, I'd rather not embarrass myself. I don't care what time I get, just so I rope that calf.

He nodded his head.

The chute flew open.

The calf bolted.

Britches galloped.

The barrier string popped open.

The rope whirled around Cody's head.

The loop floated almost in slow motion over the head of the calf.

And dropped neatly around its neck.

Britches shut it right down.

The crowd roared.

Cody left the off side of the horse, ducked under the rope, catching it in his right hand, and ran down the rope toward the stunned calf.

Use your momentum to flank the calf. Use your momentum to flank . . .

Cody reached the white-faced Hereford calf and tossed his arms over its back, grabbed onto a foreleg and hind leg, and rocked the calf back toward him.

But instead of dropping on his side in the dirt, the little Hereford kicked. Cody stumbled back and fell on the seat of his pants with the calf in his lap.

He thought he heard the crowd roar with laughter.

He thought he heard a girl scream his name.

He thought he heard the announcer say, "Uh oh!"

He knew he heard Prescott holler, "Tie that sucker!"

Shoving the calf off his legs and grabbing his pigging string from his mouth, Cody put his knee on the calf's side and grabbed two rear legs while slipping a loop around one. Then he yanked up a front hoof.

One . . . two loops and a half-hitch. Cody tossed his arms in the air, and the judge's red flag dropped.

The entire crowd rose to its feet and cheered.

Cody hustled back to Britches, who started to back away, dragging the calf.

"Don't you do that to me!" Cody called above the roar of the crowd to the cream-colored horse.

Immediately, Britches leaned forward and put slack in the rope. Cody patted his neck. "That-a-boy. Good job." He mounted the horse from the off side and rode him forward until the rope lay loose in the dirt. Then Cody stared at the calf's tied feet.

It seemed like a long time, but the judge finally signaled that the six seconds were up and the calf legally tied.

"That's a 12.2 for young Cody Clark," the announcer boomed. "With a try like that, you folks are going to watch that young man win a whole lot of rodeos someday. Thanks for the exhibition, Cody. We'll see you on down the road!"

His brothers gathered around him as he rode Britches out of the arena.

"Sorry, Prescott, I need to practice flanking a little more."

"Hey, you're the family champ," Prescott announced.

"What do you mean?"

"Me, Reno, and Denver missed our calf the first time we got in a professional rodeo."

"You did?"

"Yeah, you're the first Clark to catch a calf first try out of the box," Reno affirmed.

"I've had many times slower than 12.2," Denver added. "And I have never had a standing ovation!"

"I couldn't tell if you was ropin' that calf or just rockin' him to sleep," Eureka Blaine hooted and then slapped him on the back as he dismounted. "You done a good job, Cody Wayne. You got a good horse there. If I were you, I wouldn't ever sell him."

Cody looked at Eureka, over to his brothers, and back at Eureka. "What do you mean?"

"Two more summers of feedin' my horses, and Britches is yours. But there's no reason you cain't ride him before then. I'll give you the papers next week. That way you can pay the vet bills!"

"You're kiddin' me! I get Britches?"

"Like I said, he's too good a horse to sell. He's yours, cowboy."

Huge banks of lights mounted on towering telephone poles lit the rodeo grounds both inside and outside the arena. Cody jogged quickly around the walkway, Prescott's spurs still jingling on his boots. With his stampede string loose, his hat slipped onto his back, and his shaggy brown hair bounced as he ran.

The night air felt cool on his face. He was glad he had slipped on a long-sleeved shirt before he left home.

He trotted in front of the concession stand where two blonde-haired girls called to him. "That was totally awesome, Cody!" the taller one giggled. She was about Feather's height, but shaped more like Honey Del Mateo. She wore her hair in a ponytail. Her jeans were low at the waist, and her halter top stretched only about halfway down her front.

Cody stopped and turned to the girls. "Eh, hi! Do I know you?"

"Not yet," she giggled. "But you can visit with us at the dance after the rodeo. You are going to the dance, aren't you?"

"Nah. I don't dance."

"That's okay. We can just go for a long walk if you want to."

Cody shook his head and jogged off, the giggles of the girls fading in his ears. He kept the trot going until he reached the bleachers where his folks were sitting. As he turned to climb the steps, another girl's voice called out, "Hi, Cody!"

This time he didn't stop or turn around.

"Cody Wayne Clark, don't you run past me!"

He stopped on the first step and spun around. "Feather? What are you doing here?" She wore a long blue denim skirt with silver sequin stars on it. It hung down to her black fringed cowboy boots. She was bundled in a fleece-lined distressed leather flight jacket. Her brown hair hung straight down her back. It seemed to sparkle. Flashy gold earrings hung from her ears. It was the first time he had ever seen her wear lipstick. The eye shadow made her narrow eyes look wide, and her pale eyelids were now dark and full.

"Watching the famous Clark brothers."

"Did you see me rope?"

"Yes, and I thought you did great. What did those girls want?" Feather pointed back toward the concession stand.

"Oh . . . they just . . . they were—"

"Twelve-year-old buckle bunnies?"

"Yeah, I guess. You look nice, Feather. Are those clothes new?"

"Bruce let me pull some things out of Wardrobe. Me and Mom came over here with him. How do you like my makeup?"

"Oh, it's nice. It makes you look . . ."

"More mature?"

"Yeah. It makes you look too old to hang around a guy like me."

"Really?"

"Yeah."

"It's only temporary." She looked as several cowboys approached. "Is that Reno and Prescott with Denver?"

"Yeah. Come on up, and let's sit with my folks. Townie and Larry are here."

"I know. Mom and I were sitting with them when you roped."

"Then you know about the gym flooding?"

"Yeah. It's an answer to prayer."

"It is?"

"Yeah. We need to talk about it sometime," Feather informed him. "Maybe we could take a long walk."

Cody gave her a startled look.

"What did I say?" she stammered.

"Oh, it's just . . . That's the second time a girl—"

"Hi, Feather!" Denver called out. "Your main man did okay out there, didn't he?"

Cody jammed his hands into the front pockets of his jeans. "I'm not her—"

Feather kicked him in the ankle with the point of her boot.

"Yeah, I thought he was great!" she exclaimed.

"So we finally get to meet Cody's Feather!" Reno put his arm around her shoulder and squeezed. His black hair was about the color of his hat. He stood a couple of inches taller than Denver but was shorter than Prescott.

Cody stared at the toes of his dirty boots. "She's not my—"

Another kick to the same ankle silenced him.

"Feather darlin', I'm Prescott."

Cody always thought he looked most like Prescott, except he wasn't nearly as strong.

"And frankly," the oldest Clark brother continued, "I can't see what a purdy lady like you sees in a gangly, awkward kid like this!"

"Potential," she beamed. "He has wonderful potential."

Denver, Reno, and Prescott laughed.

"Feather's in a commercial with Bruce Baxter. That's why she has on these fancy clothes and makeup," Cody disclosed. "She doesn't usually look this way."

Denver led the others up the stairs, and Feather dropped back with Cody. "Why didn't you just tell them I'm plain and ugly without nice clothes and makeup?" she whispered.

"But that's not what I meant!"

"What did you mean, Cody Wayne?"

"I wanted them to know you're my age. I was afraid one of them might ask you to the dance after the rodeo."

Feather lifted her nose in the air. "Really? Well, maybe I should accept."

"You have to go for a walk with me, remember?"

"Yeah, you're right." They hiked up the stairs. Then Feather leaned close. "Cody, tell me the truth. Do I look sort of silly in this outfit?"

"Oh, it's okay in Spokane, but I don't think you should wear that to the first day of school at Halt Junior High."

"Whoa, cowboy," Jeremiah called out, "where did you pick up Miss America?" He and Larry howled.

"Stuff it, Yellowboy, or I'll rip your lips off!" Feather growled.

"Now that's our Feather-girl!" Larry hooted as he slid over to make room for her and Cody.

The next hour passed quickly.

In between saddle-bronc riding, steer wrestling, and a seemingly never-ending local drill team on horseback, there was talk of rodeo, basketball, horses, and girls.

When the barrel racing began, Feather leaned over to Cody. "Let's get something to eat at the concession stand."

Cody was staring at a big black thoroughbred ridden by a very young red-haired girl who was about to run the barrels.

"Nah, I'm not hungry. You go on."

"Cody!"

He turned to his right where Jeremiah sat. "You want to go to the concession stand with Feather?"

"Hey, I always want to—"

"I do not need anyone to go to the concession stand with me!" she fumed.

"But I thought—," Cody stammered.

"I want *you* to come with me! Now!" she demanded as she stomped to her feet.

"Sorry, partner," Jeremiah laughed, "I can't help you with this one!"

Cody trailed behind Feather as she descended the wooden stairs. "I told you I needed to talk to you. Well, now's the time. Right after the rodeo, Mom and I need to get back to Coeur d'Alene. We have another shoot in the morning before the sun comes up."

They strolled past the concession stand and down by the roping boxes where nervous horses and even more nervous girls now waited to race out of the darkness of a Spokane night into the bright lights and barrels of the arena.

"Do you like the acting thing?" Cody asked.

"I think I do. But this is hardly acting. I just wear this dorky costume and lay there with pizza smeared on my face," she declared.

"What did you want to talk about?"

"Can we walk over there?" She pointed to the contestant parking lot crammed with pickups, horse trailers, and travel homes.

Cody nodded and dawdled along beside her.

"There're two things. First, Bruce said if I was serious about acting and modeling, there was a school in Paris that I should attend."

"Paris? Like in Paris, France?"

"What did you think I meant—Paris, Texas?"

"But . . . but you don't just pack up and go to school in Paris!" Cody protested.

"Why not?"

"That's a—a long way away . . . and it's expensive . . . and, you know, it's a foreign country!"

"What a bright lad," she said scowling.

"What about school?"

"Mom could home-school me like she always has. Besides, Bruce has this foundation deal that gives scholarships to deserving kids, like me. Anyway, it wouldn't cost us much, and he thinks he can get Mom a job at the school, so she can go, too."

"Good ol' Bruce would do that for you?"

"I think it's a tax write-off or something like that. What do you think?"

"Well . . . it's certainly a once-in-a-lifetime opportunity I guess, but—"

"You don't want me to go, do you?"

"I didn't say that."

"But you were thinking that."

"What I was thinking was selfish."

"Me, too. That's why I already turned down the deal," Feather announced.

"Really?"

"Actually, my mom turned down the deal."

"No foolin'? Why did she do that?"

"She said she'd been to Paris, and it wasn't all that big a deal. She said I was too young, that I should wait ten years to do something like that, and . . ."

"And what?"

"And that in her entire life she had never had friends as good as you and Larry and Townie, and it would be foolish of me to leave all of you."

"Hey, Cody!" a young girl's voice sing-songed from the shadows next to a horse trailer.

Cody stared through the darkness to see the outline of a girl standing with a boy who was leaning against the trailer.

"Yeah?"

"Where did you find the snotty debutante?" came the giggling reply.

"In a Bruce Baxter film," Cody called back.

"Really?" the boy in the shadows replied.

Cody and Feather kept walking through the parked rigs. She tugged on Cody's coat sleeve.

"Never in my life have I ever been called a snotty debutante!" she whispered. "I've been called a hippie, white trash, an eco-freak, and some names that you see written on gas station bathroom walls, but never a snotty debutante. Was that one of your little buckle bunnies?"

"I don't know who she is. She's weird. Did you know she wears a silver ring in her pierced, eh, her . . ."

"Her pierced what?" Feather demanded.

"Her pierced belly button!"

"You've never seen that before?"

Cody shook his head.

"Good."

"So you're really not going to Paris?" Cody pursued.

"Of course not."

"I'm glad."

"I know." She traipsed over to a stock trailer and peeked through the aluminum slats into the darkness. "Hey, there's a horse in here!"

"You expecting a camel?" He leaned against the side of the trailer next to her. In the background they could hear the crowd cheering. "What was the other thing you wanted to talk about?"

Feather took a deep breath and let it out slowly. "Okay, here's the deal. I need you to hear me out on this. The other night I laid awake trying to decide whether to film this commercial or stay and play in the basketball tournament. I wanted to do both so bad it hurt me. Finally, I struck a deal about daylight."

"What kind of a deal?"

"I told God if He could provide a way that I could play in the tournament *and* make the commercial, then I'd know He was speaking to me, and I'd better get serious with Jesus. Well, all day yesterday nothing happened, and I figured my prayer wasn't being answered. But now . . . I'll be able to play in the championship game after all. It's like God kept His part of the bargain, and I'm forced to keep mine."

"You mean, you don't want to believe in Jesus, but you feel obligated?" Cody pressed.

"No, that's not it . . . really . . . but I was just . . . maybe I shouldn't have made that kind of deal."

"I think the Lord wants us to believe because it's true, not because He does something we ask Him to do."

"So what should I do now?"

"Keep your promise," Cody advised.

"But I thought you said—"

"Jesus is real, and you made a promise. Now you have two reasons for believing."

"How come you make it sound so simple? Cody, this is scary to me."

"I don't know very much really. Maybe you should talk to my mom. But the Lord's real in my life. That's about all I can say."

The roar from the crowd increased.

Feather stepped out from the shadows and peered toward the lit arena. "What's happening in there now?"

"Bull-riding, from the sound of it."

"Is that the last event?"

"Yep."

"We'd better get back. We're riding back to Coeur d'Alene in Bruce's black stretch limo Hummer."

"He's got a stretch limo Hummer?"

"Yeah, is that wild, or what?"

They walked past empty roping boxes and the concession stand.

"Will you be home in time for a game tomorrow night—
I mean, if we have a game?" Cody asked.

"I'll be there. Have you determined how to beat J. J.
and this guy Ty?"

"I'd like to keep from getting my arm broken."

"Larry will figure something out."

"He's still stunned from missing a shot last night,"
Cody added.

"He'll bounce back," she giggled.

"He's already thinking about next summer. He says
we'll have an awesome team next year!"

"I'm going to play in the girls' league next year,"
Feather announced.

"Why?"

"Because I'm a girl."

"But you're on our team!"

"I'll come to all your games."

"Why do you want to switch?"

"Because in the boys' league, I'm just another one of
the competitors. But in the girls' league, I could be a star."

Cody stared out into the arena where the pick-up men
were trying to herd a 2,000-pound "Brahma" bull out an
open gate. "It won't be the same without you on the team,"
he said finally.

"Things change, Cody."

"Why? I like things the way they are."

"What if you find out you like things different, too?
This summer was different from last summer, right?"

"Yeah," he admitted.

"Change can be good."

"I guess so."

"In fact, I'd like to change right now," Feather insisted.

"You would?"

"Yeah. I'd like to change out of these clothes and put on some shorts and a tie-dyed T-shirt. Tell me the truth—I look dorky in these, don't I?"

"Oh, not dorky. But maybe . . . like I said . . . over-dressed. It's sort of the way seniors in high school dress."

"They dress like this?"

"Like for a dance or something."

"Good. Now I'll know what to wear when you ask me to go with you to the senior prom. You are going to ask me to the senior prom, aren't you?"

"Prom? Man, that's . . . that's five years away!"

"Four and a half. Are you going to ask me to the senior prom or not?" she pressed.

"Eh . . . yeah, but I've never—"

"Of course you've never asked anyone before. You're only thirteen."

"But I can't . . . I don't know how to dance," Cody admitted.

"You've got five years to learn. Are you going to ask me or not?"

"Eh, yeah . . . I guess so."

"Good. I accept," Feather replied. "What time will you be by in your black Dodge pickup to pick me up?"

"A black Dodge pickup?"

"That's what you'll drive, isn't it?"

Cody pushed his hat back. "Well . . . I hope so, but that's a long time."

"You didn't tell me what time you'd be by," she insisted.

"That's five years from now. How would I know?"

"Four and a half. I'll wear something in rose pink, so buy me some flowers to match. I think a black western tux would look good on you, especially with your black cowboy hat. Let's say you pick me up at 5:00, we drive to Lewiston for an elegant supper, and then we go back up to Halt for the dance. How does that sound?"

"How in the world would I know? I won't remember all of this for five years!"

Feather fidgeted with her gold dangling earrings. "I'll remind you."

"But what if . . . I change my mind or something?"

"You can't."

"Why?"

"Because cowboys always keep their promises! It's part of the Code of the West, right?"

"Yeah. Well . . . how about you? What if you change your mind?"

"I can't."

"Why?"

"It's part of the code," she giggled.

"What code?" he demanded.

"The Code of Snotty Debutantes!"

Seven

Cody fastened the top button on his long-sleeved pullover black shirt. A stiff, cool wind blew around the corner of the building. The few high clouds reflected almost orange from the setting Idaho sun. "Townie, tell me what your mom said when you talked to her."

"She said Two Ponies and Sweetwater were both conscious and visiting with some cute nurses. They even let them stay in the same intensive care room. She said the doctors aren't talking survival anymore; they're talking recovery. She was really encouraged."

"Did she mention your moving to Denver with her?" Cody asked.

"She said she won't consider that for a few more weeks. So you guys are stuck with me, cowboy. Halt's the only school I've ever gone to. I can't imagine going anywhere else. And I can't believe it starts tomorrow." Jeremiah shoved the sleeves of his black Chicago Bulls sweatshirt up to his elbows and took a deep swig from his Mountain Dew.

"I can't believe I'm actually going to attend classes!" Feather reached down and brushed a thread off her new jeans. "I'm thirteen years old and going to school for the very first time. I just know I'll do something stupid, and everyone will think I'm a dork. I've never even had to sit at a desk in my life. Can I sit by you guys?"

Cody leaned his head back against the wall and closed his eyes. "Not in first period. Mr. Aaron teaches history, and we have assigned seating."

"Last spring I did my studies sitting cross-legged on a buffalo hide in the middle of a tepee. Now I have assigned seating. How does he do it? Alphabetically?" Feather quizzed.

"Nope," Cody explained. "It's all random, and he changes it every month. But not all teachers are that way. I bet Miss DeGarcia lets us sit anywhere we want to in health. Come to think about it, don't sit next to me in health."

"Why?"

"Because those work sheets can be embarrassing!" Jeremiah whooped. "But we can sit wherever we want in English. Hey, when Mrs. Fletcher asks us to write about what we did this summer, what will you say?"

Larry Lewis dribbled his basketball back and forth on the crumbling concrete slab in front of them. "You know what I'm going to write about? I'm going to write how we wasted our time in front of the Buy Rite Market with the championship game only two hours away! What are we doing sitting around here?"

"Relaxing," Jeremiah proclaimed. "Hanging loose.

Letting the tiredness and tension drain from our practice-weary bodies so we can play at peak performance when it really matters."

Cody stretched his arms. "I thought we were just avoiding the subject of basketball so we wouldn't have to think about J. J. and Ty."

Jeremiah tossed up a blue peanut M & M and caught it in his open mouth. "That, too."

"We should be reviewing game plans," Larry insisted.

"Did that this afternoon," Jeremiah countered.

"And run through some new plays."

"Did that this morning," Cody reminded him.

"Feather didn't. She just got home an hour ago."

"I'm a quick learner. Relax, Larry!"

"Relax?"

Jeremiah stretched out his legs in front of him. "Yeah. You remember how to relax, don't you? Remember how peaceful it was when we tubed down the Clearwater that afternoon?"

"I was terrified by the rapids!" Larry admitted.

"Or how about when we went horseback riding?" Feather suggested. "Remember the wildflowers?"

"I remember getting bucked off twice. You call that relaxing?"

"How about down in the canyon at Mr. Levine's cabin? Now that was absolutely relaxing," Cody offered.

"You mean when those murdering dope pushers burst in and threatened to kill us?"

"Larry, didn't you do anything relaxing all summer?"

"Basketball. I relax when I'm playing basketball."

"How about when Lanni DeLira went over to your house and you showed her your basketball card collection? That must have been relaxing," Cody pressed.

"Are you kidding? I was so nervous I almost . . ." Larry looked over at Feather and then clamped his mouth shut.

"You almost what?" she pressed.

"Nothing!"

Feather pulled her long braid around and laid it under her nose like a mustache. "Hey, you guys! Guess what book Bruce Baxter has on his dressing room bookshelf."

"How much time did you spend in his dressing room?" Cody asked.

Feather giggled. "Cody's cute when he's jealous, isn't he?"

"Oh, brother!" Larry groaned. "I'm going home and shoot some hoops."

"Wait," Feather called, "just wait until I tell you about this book. It's called the *History of the Camas Prairie*."

"By Dr. Spencer?"

"Yes."

"He was my dad's history teacher," Cody explained.

"Well, then, you might know that it says that in 1897 a merchant by the name of H. M. Holt applied for a post office permit. He wanted to call the new settlement Holt. But the district director misread the application and wrote down Halt. From then on, that's what the town has been called."

"A misspelled word? And to think of all those things you tried to tell me all summer," Larry moaned. "I'm going to shoot hoops. Let's meet at the gym at 6:00."

"The game doesn't start until 7:00," Jeremiah reminded him.

"Please! Humor me a little," Larry pleaded.

"Only if you bring a plate of your lucky brownies," Jeremiah teased.

"Hey, it's better than that! Mom baked me some lucky chocolate eclairs!"

"All right!" Jeremiah shouted. "Maybe we should show up at five o'clock!"

"We can't eat them until after the game."

"Why do we need luck after the game?" Cody pressed.

"For our bones to heal quickly!" Jeremiah hooted.

"Let's have a party after the game," Feather suggested.

"Win or lose?" Larry asked.

"Yep," Cody replied. "Let's meet at our house. I'll furnish the drinks."

"I'll bring some chips!" Jeremiah offered.

"And I'll bring some carrot strips and vegetable dip!" Feather announced.

All three boys glared at her.

"Eh . . . I won't bring very many."

Cody wore thin white cotton gloves as he tossed his rope over the plastic steer head in the backyard. Denver jogged down the back steps of the house and out to him.

"I'm going to pick up Becky, and we're coming to your game."

"It's two hours away."

"Good. That'll give us some time to visit." Denver

revealed the dual dimples that set off his smile like quotation marks.

"I thought Mom and Dad would be home by now."

"Yeah, me too. They probably took Grandma and Grandpa shopping on the way home," Denver suggested.

"Did you have any supper?"

Denver glanced at his wristwatch. "If I hustle, I'll probably get invited to eat at Becky's. Mom's probably bringing you home a pizza or something."

"I don't think I'll eat until after the game."

"You nervous?"

"Yeah," Cody admitted. "We haven't beaten the Prairie Pirates all year, so I shouldn't worry about that. But this is the first time I've played against Ty, J. J.'s cousin."

"You can take him, lil' bro'. No matter how tough he is, he can't kick harder than a calf or bite worse than a horse. You proved yourself cowboy-tough this summer."

Cody was still roping when he saw the headlights of the Clark Suburban turn into the dirt alley and roll to a stop behind the house. He quickly coiled his rope as his parents climbed out.

"Hey, Mom! You guys are late. I've got to be at the gym in about twenty minutes. Larry wants us there early. You know how nervous he gets before a game. Anyway, I invited them over for a little party afterwards, but you don't have to fix anything because the others are bringing the food. I told them we'd furnish drinks. Did you bring me any pizza?"

"For heaven's sake, Cody," his mother snapped, "be quiet!"

Cody stood in the fading darkness of early September and stared as his mother ran into house. He felt a strong arm around his shoulder.

"Dad . . . is Mom crying?"

"I reckon she is, Cody."

"But . . . but why? What did I say? I've never seen her cry except during some old movie on television."

"It's been a rough afternoon." Cody and his dad sat down on the concrete step that faced a grassless backyard and a dirt alley. "I wasn't going to tell you this until after your game. But Mama took it hard, and maybe it's best you know now."

Cody's stomach felt like it had dropped to his ankles. "What is it? What's going on?"

"We went to the doctor with Grandma and Grandpa."

"Is it Grandpa?"

Mr. Clark put his hand on Cody's knee. "He's got cancer."

"But . . . but he's hardly sick or anything." Cody could feel the tears sliding down his cheeks.

"It's prostate cancer."

"They can treat that, can't they?"

"They've got him scheduled for some surgery, but it's pretty advanced. The doc wasn't optimistic."

"But they've got all this medicine and treatment and stuff. He'll be all right, Dad, won't he?"

"Cody, you know I can't lie to you. I never have. I won't

now. Chances are, Grandpa won't last much past Christmas."

"We can pray. The Lord can heal him!"

"Yes, He can. Maybe that's the way it will turn out. But it seems to me it's a whole lot more important to accept the Lord's will than to try to twist His arm to accept our will. Now let's just take it one day at a time and see what happens."

"How are Grandma and Grandpa doing?"

"Grandpa said they've gone through rough times before. They figure it's just another one of those times."

Neither spoke for a moment.

"Is Mom going to be all right?"

"She's a strong woman. . . . She'll pull through. But I reckon right now Mama would like a big hug from her youngest. It won't hurt if she sees those tears either."

Cody wiped his eyes on his shirt and sniffed, "I'm not crying, really!"

"Well, I am. So get in there and give your mom a hug. Right about now, she's feelin' mighty low about snapping at you."

It was 6:22 when Cody walked into the Halt High School gym, wearing navy blue basketball shorts and an orange tie-dyed sleeveless T-shirt under his black warm-up suit. His dark glasses covered his eyes. High in the crowded bleachers he spotted three other matching tie-dyed shirts, one of whose wearers carried a basketball and paced back and forth.

Cody wove up through the crowd, tossed his gear bag down next to Jeremiah, and plopped down on the last row with his back against the wall.

"Hey, cool dude," Jeremiah laughed, "what's with the shades?"

"I thought we agreed to be here early," Larry began. "We had a little net time at 6:00. Now it's too late. I thought you said—"

"Cody Wayne," Feather interrupted, "have you been crying?"

He looked away from them and studied the girls' championship game that was taking place on the west end of the gym.

"Really, Cody, what's wrong?" she insisted.

Lord, I don't really want to talk about it. I don't want to think about it. I want this day to go away. It's a mulligan. Everyone ought to have one or two days that they can throw away. This is mine. This day does not exist in the history of the world. All the sorrow and pain should be taken away, and Grandpa is free from cancer. Please, Lord, heal him today!

"Cody? Are you just going to sit there and ignore us?" Feather insisted.

"Clark, I think you owe the team an explanation!" Larry Lewis ranted.

Cody tugged off his dark glasses. He could feel the tears roll down his cheeks. "My granddad has cancer and will probably die within the next six months!" he blurted out.

Panicked grief spread across Larry's face, and he

immediately sat down and buried his head in his hands. Jeremiah looked straight down at his shoes. Cody noticed his tears puddle next to his feet.

Feather took a deep breath, rubbed her nose, and bit her lip. She didn't cry. "I don't have any idea what it's like to lose grandparents. I've never even met mine once."

The word *once* seemed to be the trigger. Suddenly tears streamed past her freckles and down her smooth, thin cheeks.

Cody scooted down one row between Feather and Jeremiah, but no one said anything. Finally he leaned back to where Larry still sat with head in hands.

"You thinking about your granddad, L. B.?"

"Yeah, it still hurts. I'm sorry I got mad at you, Cody. It seems pretty stupid now. If you want to go on home, go ahead," Larry suggested.

Feather scooted around on the bleacher behind Cody. She began rubbing his shoulders and neck. "Can you imagine Larry Bird Lewis saying that two months ago?"

Larry moved over next to Cody, and Feather rotated, rubbing all three boys' shoulders.

"I don't feel too much like playing basketball," Larry admitted.

"Larry's sick," Townie teased, and Feather turned her attention to his broad shoulders.

"I'm serious, guys," Larry continued. "I'm tired of being tense. It's not just Cody's granddad. It's my granddad's death last spring. And my mom getting pregnant. And Feather's dad off in Dixie with some other woman. And maybe she's moving to Paris. And Townie's brothers in critical condition. And the first day of a new school tomorrow. I don't need the tension of this championship game—you know what I mean?"

Cody looked at Feather, then at Jeremiah. He wiped his eyes and released a deep sigh, then jokingly put his hands around Larry's neck. "All right, buddy, who are you really, and what did you do with our friend Larry Bird Lewis?"

"It's a conspiracy, man!" Jeremiah chuckled.

"We want our Larry Bird Lewis back, and we want him right now!" Feather clutched Larry's ears.

"Really?" Larry croaked.

"We want the greatest under-sixteen-year-old basketball mind on the face of the planet to come back and help us win this championship!" Cody announced.

"But we don't want to put any pressure on him," Feather added.

"Are you guys serious?"

"The Squad has one more game to play," Jeremiah insisted.

"Okay, but I meant what I said."

"Thanks, Larry." Cody released his grip, and Feather began to rub Larry's neck.

"Now, Capt. Lewis, how are we going to play them close and still be relaxed?" Cody challenged.

Larry wiped his eyes on the tail of his shirt.

"Let's put a half-court press on them from the start. In-your-face defense. We'll rotate in the fourth person on every made basket, and we'll switch off whoever we're guarding every time we sub. The fresh guy goes to guard Ty every time."

"How about offense?" Cody quizzed.

"Forget the plays. Everyone is responsible for getting us five points. That's it," Larry proclaimed. "Just go get us five points any way you can."

"What about when they clobber us?" Jeremiah probed.

"Everyone laughs," Larry suggested. "If any one of us gets creamed, we all laugh. It's the exact opposite of what they're expecting. I can guarantee you that they haven't practiced what to do if we start laughing at their strong-arm tactics."

"Let me get this straight," Cody repeated. "All we have to remember is press them every play, get five points each . . . and laugh a lot?"

"Yeah, what do you think?"

"I think you're brilliant!" Feather declared.

Larry glanced around without smiling. "I am good, aren't I?"

After team introductions and a short speech by Mr. Lewis, Larry and J. J. Melton were summoned to the free-throw line for the coin toss.

"Take my place, cowboy!" Larry called. "I am kicking back and relaxing!"

Cody met J. J. at the line and reached out to shake his hand. The offer was refused.

"Keep out of our way, Clark," J. J. muttered beneath his breath. "Or you'll be starting school in a cast."

Press . . . five points each . . . laugh.

Cody stood real close to J. J., their noses only inches apart. Cody smiled from ear to ear. "I call heads."

J. J. took a step backwards, but Cody followed him, still in his face. Melton put his hands on Cody's chest and shoved him backwards. Cody took two steps back, stumbled, and landed with a thud on the seat of his pants.

Press . . . five points each . . . laugh.

Just as Cody began to laugh, so did the rest of the Lewis and Clark Squad.

"What are you freaks laughing about? We won the toss!" J. J. shouted.

Two things Cody knew for sure about Ty. He was the biggest kid to ever attend Halt Junior High. He was seven inches taller than Cody and at least fifty pounds heavier. And in the short time Ty had been in his class, Cody never knew of a time that he got a grade higher than an F. It was reported that Ty often carried a switchblade knife to school, but Cody doubted the story. There was no reason for him to bring a knife. He could have beaten every kid into the ground with his fists.

Feather sat out the first play. Larry guarded Devin. Jeremiah took J. J., and Cody was left with Ty. Devin took the inbound pass from J. J., but with Larry in his face, he dumped it off to Ty at the free-throw line. Ty lumbered toward the basket, running right over the top of Cody.

Cody crashed to the floor, and Townie started to laugh. Ty's dribble bounced off Cody's elbow, shooting a sharp pain up to his neck. He caught his breath and tried to join the Squad in the laughter.

Meanwhile, the ball squirted sideways. Larry dove under Devin's arms and scooped the ball up and flipped it to Jeremiah all in one motion. Jeremiah glanced at his shoes behind the three-point line and sailed the ball from the south corner of the floor.

Nothing but net.

"All right!" Jeremiah yelled. "I got three of mine! Come in for me, Feather!"

Feather guarded Ty. Cody scooted over to Devin. And Larry was on J. J. When J. J. tried tossing the ball in to Devin, Larry jumped high and blocked it right back to J. J. who, reacting to protect himself, caught the ball.

"Our ball!" Larry yelled.

"You hit it out!" J. J. protested.

"But you caught it with your feet out of bounds! It's ours."

"You think you can take it from me?" J. J. growled.

"It's their ball," Devin called over.

J. J. refused to hand the ball to Larry. He let it drop and roll toward the bleachers.

First Feather, then the others, began to laugh.

"What's so funny?" Ty boomed.

"Basketball is a fun sport, don't you think?" Feather replied gaily. "We enjoy the game, that's all."

"You're all a bunch of weirdos!"

The Lewis and Clark Squad howled with more laughter.

In the midst of the celebration, Larry bounced the ball to Cody, who whipped it over to Feather. Ty threw one big, hairy arm around her neck in an attempt to swat the ball.

Feather leaned over and kissed Ty's arm. He jerked away from her, and she drove in for an uncontested lay-in.

"There's two for me," she reported.

"You can't do that!" J. J. hollered. "She tried to bite Ty. . . . She tried to bite!"

"She kissed me. That's what she did." Ty rubbed his arm as if to remove the remnants of the kiss.

"Well, that's sort of like a bite!" J. J. complained. "You guys aren't playing fair!"

"But we're having fun!" Feather insisted.

"And we're winning 5 to zip," Larry chuckled.

The Squad rotated.

Pressed on every play.

Laughed.

Really laughed.

While the Pirates fumed.

Plowed into people.

Yelled.

Hacked.

Shoved.

Elbowed.

Tripped.

Then the Squad sprawled.

Limped.

Staggered.

Winced.

But kept on laughing.

When the Pirates took their first lead at 16 to 15, Larry called time-out.

"We're keeping it close!" he boasted.

"We're getting beat to a pulp," Jeremiah moaned.

Feather started to giggle.

"You don't have to do that now," Larry reminded her.

"No, really," she continued, "I can't help myself. This is the funniest thing I ever did in my life. Look at me! I've got bruises all over me! If this happened in the park, someone would be arrested for assault. Only the idiots on the Squad would do this!"

Jeremiah joined her in laughter.

Cody held his face in his left hand. "I'd laugh, but I think Ty broke my jaw with his elbow."

"Really?" Larry quizzed.

"No, but it does hurt. What now, coach?"

"I think we pushed the laughing, have-fun game plan as far as it will go. We should try something different."

"No!" Cody protested. "If we're still laughing when this game is over, then we won, no matter what the score. It means we played our game, set the pace, and had fun. Even if we lose, folks will go around town saying, 'Hey, did you see the Lewis and Clark Squad last night?' If we come out all serious and lose, they'll just talk about the Pirates."

Larry shook his head. "We won't score another point this way."

"Sure we will," Cody insisted. "I need three more, and you need two. Let's push it to the end."

Larry grinned. "This is crazy. Bobby Knight would never do it this way! Ty's guarding me, so Cody you take your best three-pointer."

"I don't have a good three-pointer, and you know it. Larry, take a jumper over Ty."

"I can't shoot over him. No one can shoot over him."

"No one's tried. Come on, Larry, you have the quickest release on the prairie. Back into the free-throw line and do that little spin jumper."

"You're the man," Jeremiah concurred.

"If he blocks it back at me, I'm dead."

"We promise we'll laugh if he blocks it," Feather encouraged him.

"So will everyone else in the gym. Are you guys sure about this?"

Cody nodded.

Cody bounced it in to Larry, who backed the massive Ty to the line. Larry's jumper came as a surprise to everyone on the Pirate team, especially to Ty, who never got his hands in the air and almost blocked the shot with his forehead.

But he didn't.

Nothing but net. Larry threw his head back to the ceiling and howled in laughter.

"With hands that quick, you should have been a gunfighter," Cody teased.

"I could have roamed the West as Larry the Kid!"

"Now that is really funny!" Jeremiah chuckled as he trotted out and allowed Feather back in.

Larry guarded J. J., who was bringing the ball in. This time J. J. faked a pass, and Larry jumped straight up with his hands raised. Only four feet away from Larry, J. J. then slammed a hard overhand pass right into Larry's stomach.

Larry crumpled to the floor.

The crowd groaned.

Feather and Cody ran to Larry's side.

J. J. stepped inbound, picked up the loose ball, and dribbled in for an uncontested lay-in.

Cody was on his knees. "Can you breathe?"

Larry shook his head back and forth.

"Townie, call our last time-out," Cody hollered to the sidelines.

"No!" Larry managed to gasp. "Laugh."

"What?"

"Laugh!"

"It's not funny," Cody insisted.

"Laugh!"

Cody could see tears in the corners of Larry's eyes.

Then Cody and Feather began to laugh.

"Don't call time-out, Townie; call 911!" Cody shouted.

The crowd roared as Larry staggered to the sidelines and Jeremiah returned to the game.

Devin walked off the court. J. J. screamed at his departing teammate, "Devin, where are you going?"

"Home!" he yelled back. "I don't want to play that kind of ball anymore, J. J."

"Get back here!" J. J. screamed.

"Get real, J. J. That's not basketball you're playing. It's revenge."

"I believe it's a tie game, and it's our ball," Cody announced.

Larry stood at the sidelines doubled over, still gasping for air. "It's your shot, cowboy. Win it for us."

"Yellowboy has to go out!" J. J. hollered.

"Why?"

"He has blood on his leg. He has to sit out a play and get the bleeding stopped."

Jeremiah looked down at the red streak on his brown leg and began to laugh. "That's a good sign. I still have blood! You have to come in for me, L. B."

"I can't . . ."

"Sure you can. It's cowboy's shot anyway." Jeremiah trotted to the sidelines.

Ty and J. J. abandoned the staggering Larry Lewis and guarded Cody and Feather.

"You kiss me again, and I'll bust your head open," Ty growled at Feather.

"I bet you say that to all the girls!" Feather quipped.

Cody tossed the ball to Feather, who fired it right back to him. He decided to use the reeling Larry Lewis for a pick and drove near him.

J. J. lowered his shoulder and crashed into Larry, sending him sprawling behind the three-point line. He sat on the floor, with eyes wide and mouth dropped open.

J. J. was on top of Cody, who couldn't even see past Ty to find Feather. Cody rolled the ball back out to the sitting Larry Lewis.

"Sling one up there, Larry the Kid!" Cody shouted.

Larry grabbed the ball and, with a right-handed overhand throw, slammed it as far as he could from his sitting position.

Nothing but glass.

And rim.

And net!

Larry collapsed on his back and shouted, "Yes!"

After that, the gym went wild. Nobody remembered anything until four battered basketball players sat on the floor of the Clark family living room, staring at four of the largest chocolate eclairs known to mankind.

"I can't move," Larry gasped. "Would someone put that eclair in my mouth and push my lips up and down."

"Larry, you look good in black and blue. They're your colors!" Feather teased.

"Thank you, thank you very much," Larry mumbled.

"That was the most fun I ever had getting beat up! And your winning shot just might be the most dramatic in the history of Halt basketball!" Cody added.

"Man, I wish we had it on video! Would that be cool, or what?" Larry licked a thick globule of chocolate off his lips. "If we have to write one of those summer vacation papers, I'm going to call it 'My Championship Summer.'"

"Not me." Jeremiah's smile was wider than the eclair in his hand.

"Oh?" Feather teased. "Are you going to call it your 'DeVonne Summer'?"

"No way. I'll call mine 'The Eagle Song.'"

"What about you, Feather-girl?" Larry inquired.

"That's easy. It's my 'Summer of Transformation.'"

"Huh?" Jeremiah queried. "Is that a . . . girl thing?"

"Girl thing! My dad moves off. My mom gets us a house in town. I quit being a strict vegetarian. I play in a boys' basketball league, make two commercials with Bruce Baxter, make new friends, and go from doubting God's existence to believing in Jesus. I'd say that was some change, wouldn't you?"

"Oh, yeah," Jeremiah gulped, "that change!"

"How about Cody Wayne?" Feather asked. "What are you going to call your report?"

"I think I'll call mine 'The World's Fastest Summer.' I don't think I was bored for thirty seconds all summer. It sure went out with a . . . bang!"

"And a thud," Feather added.

"And a crunch!" Larry concurred.

"That was the weirdest game I ever played in my life," Townie admitted. Whipped cream trickled down the corner of his lips.

"Well, the game's over, basketball's over . . . summer's over," Cody sighed.

"You know what would be totally cool? How would you guys like this to be the first day of summer vacation, and we could do it all over again?" Larry asked.

Cody looked at Jeremiah and Feather, then back to Larry.

In unison they replied. "No way!"

For a list of other books by
Stephen Bly
or information regarding speaking engagements
write:
Stephen Bly
Winchester, Idaho 83555